The Phantom Unicorn

Zetta Elliott

The Phantom Unicorn

Pictures by Charity Russell

Rosetta
Press

for Lucy,
who never sneered

1

When the phone rings, I quickly get up from the kitchen table and scrape my leftovers into the compost bin. Ma made crispy shrimp dumplings for dinner—my favorite—but I'm not that hungry tonight.

"Can you get that for me, Qing Yuan?"

Ma's got Sophie on her hip but she can still answer the phone. Ever since my baby sister was born, Ma's learned to do a lot of things with just one hand. Normally I'd help her out, but I know it's my dad calling and I don't want to talk to him right now. So instead I rinse my plate and put it in the dishwasher. Ma grabs the phone and tucks it between her ear and her shoulder. When she tries to get my attention, I pretend not to notice and head to my room. I close the door behind me but leave it open just a crack so I can hear what she's telling my dad.

"I'm really sorry, Jaleel. I guess he's just not ready. Try calling again tomorrow. No, no—it's not your fault. You did the right thing. I'll talk to him. He'll understand—he just needs a little more time."

I close the door the rest of the way and go over to my model castles. I've got five now, each one different from all the others. Dad sent me the latest one for my birthday. It's got real water in the moat and a drawbridge that you can crank up and down. I was looking forward to showing it to Dad this week, but then he got arrested and all our plans went out the window.

Mama's in Maryland at her field lab. We moved all the way across the country for her to take a job at a university here in New York, but as soon as we got here, she split. Mama's a marine biologist. She's only got a few weeks each year to study these crabs that lay their eggs in the marshes around Chesapeake Bay.

Ma has Sophie to keep her busy and she's already got clients coming by even though we just moved in last week. This weekend was supposed to be all about me and Dad. We both live on the east coast now, which means we don't have to get on a plane whenever we want to see each other. But being in New York doesn't mean much if my dad's behind bars.

My parents always tell me to do the right thing and I really do try. I don't complain when Sophie tears up my comic books, 'cause she's just a baby and doesn't know any better. And I don't get mad when strangers come up to me and ask, "What *are* you?"

Back in Berkeley there were lots of kids who looked like me—and lots of families that were just like mine. I've only been in Washington Heights for a few days, but so far I haven't seen anybody like us. And when Mama comes back from Maryland, people are going to stare even more. She's Black but Ma's Asian. When we go out together, some folks think she's my nanny. I can speak Mandarin but I have an Afro. That seems to confuse a lot of people.

Mama says our family is *ours*—we don't have to make sense to anyone else. Ma says, "Just be yourself." Dad says, "Hold your head up and make your ancestors proud." They all met when they were in college. I guess they had a blast because they're always smiling in the photos I've seen. My folks don't remember what it's like to be a fifth grader. I start a new school in a couple of weeks. I had a lot of friends back home, but we're not in Berkeley anymore.

If Dad had come up to New York, I could've had a few days of feeling like a normal regular kid (we don't use that "n-word" in my family). My eyes are like Ma's, but Dad's hair is like mine and our skin's just about the same shade of brown. We're both into the Middle Ages and he was going to take me to The Cloisters—this medieval museum that's within walking distance of our new home. But none of that's going to happen now.

The phone rings again and a few moments later I hear the doorbell ring. When Ma knocks on my bedroom door, I say, "Come in," but I don't turn around. Instead I snap one of the turrets off my latest model castle and crumble it into the tiny grey blocks that came in the box.

"This just arrived. It's for you," Ma says.

I don't want to turn around but my curiosity gets the better of me. I set down the turret and look at the yellow envelope in Ma's outstretched hand. Sophie reaches for it, too, but Ma tells her, "That isn't for you, darling. It's for your brother."

First I read the return address. It's from Thandie, my dad's girlfriend. Then I tear open the padded envelope and look inside. There's a crumpled piece of paper and something shiny. I toss the letter on my bed and dump the round object into my hand. It's a small round mirror—two mirrors back-to-back held together by a metal circle. It's not easy to see my reflection in either one because the mirrors have a weathered look. A piece of string runs through a small loop coming out of the mirror's gold rim. On a round paper tag someone has written, "A looking drop for past, present, and future."

I hold up the weird mirror and frown. "Dad sent me a Christmas tree ornament?"

Sophie reaches for the mirror with both hands as it twirls on the string. Mama sometimes calls her "Magpie" because she likes shiny things.

Ma tries to smile at me but I can tell she's confused by Dad's strange gift, too. But instead of trying to find an explanation, she changes the subject. "Why don't we go to The Cloisters tomorrow—just us?"

Ma doesn't mean just me and her. She means me, her, *and* Sophie. I wanted to visit the museum with my dad. It won't be the same if Ma takes me. I love my little sister but babies are like Godzilla—they ruin a lot of things whether they mean to or not. It's their nature.

I glance at the unread letter on my bed and then turn back to my castles. "You don't have to do that," I say. "I'll just hang out here tomorrow."

Ma comes over and puts her free hand on my shoulder. "I know I don't have to—I *want* to. It'll be fun! And we need to get you out of the house. There's a cafe at the museum—we could have lunch there, if you like. And then…"

I tense and Ma takes her hand off my shoulder. "I know you're angry, Qing Yuan, and disappointed. Maybe tomorrow we can talk about what's going on with your dad. Okay?"

When I just shrug, Ma bends down and kisses me on the cheek. "Don't stay up too late," she whispers in my ear. "I love

you."

I know I should say, "I love you, too, Ma," but I don't. I could turn around, wrap my arms around her waist, and give her a hug. She could only hug me back with one arm, but even that would make me feel better right now. But I don't do that. I stay silent and wait for Ma to close the door behind her. Then I listen until I hear her walk across the apartment's creaky wood floors. When I'm sure she's in her own room, I slide my fingers under the thin base supporting my newest castle. Then I flip the base as high as I can, sending the model castle flying into the wall. The castle shatters into pieces.

I don't bother to read Dad's letter. Instead I crush the wrinkled sheet of paper into a ball and throw it on the floor. Then I fall onto my bed and cry myself to sleep.

2

"Are you heading to the museum? Oh, my goodness—your little girl is *adorable*!"

This is how it always happens—how I become a ghost. We'll be standing on the sidewalk (waiting for the bus, in this case) and a woman will walk by and feel compelled to say something to Ma. Maybe she's pushing a stroller or toting around her own baby in a carrier like the one Ma wears. Either way, they'll start chatting like they're old friends instead of total strangers, and that's when I disappear from view. It's like there's a club for mothers, which is kind of cool, really. Except I'm not a mother, so I'm not part of the club.

Today we're waiting for the bus that will drop us off right in front of the Cloisters. A woman pushing a sandy-haired toddler in a jogger's stroller smiles at us, and then stops to peer at Sophie. I'm biased, of course, but my sister is a super cute baby. She's got sparkling black eyes, long eyelashes, and a halo of glossy black curls. I looked a lot like Sophie when I was a baby, and Mama says people always stopped to admire me, too. So I'm not surprised that people notice my sister and stop to get a better look. But right now,

I just want to get a better look at the medieval artifacts in the museum.

"It's a quick walk to the Cloisters," the woman tells Ma. "I'm heading that way myself—I'd be happy to show you the way."

Ma thanks the woman, they take a moment to exchange names, and then they start walking away. With Clare's stroller, the sidewalk is only wide enough for two adults so I lag behind. No one seems to notice. The mothers club is officially in session and I am officially invisible.

The path that leads to the museum winds through Fort Tryon Park. Tall trees dot the grassy meadow that extends all the way to the Hudson River. I know that because Clare's talking nonstop. She points out the dog run and advises Ma to use the bike lane in the road since cycling can be tricky on the narrow, hilly paths. I hope that Clare and her kid don't decide to join us for a tour of the museum. She's a nice lady, but I guess I'm a little bit jealous. Why is it so easy for grown-ups to make friends?

Ma's pumping Clare for information about the schools and shops in our new neighborhood. Every so often they turn and smile at me to make me feel included in their conversation, but I'm not interested in the best place to buy gluten-free bread.

I reach into my pocket and wrap my fingers around the looking drop. I'm not sure why I brought it with me. Dad's letter is in my other pocket. I finally read it this morning and I don't feel as angry as I was last night. In fact, I feel a little bit guilty. I'm here in a lush green park, heading to a museum full of my favorite things, and my dad's stuck in a cramped jail cell. I don't know that it's cramped, but from what I've seen on TV, jail cells aren't usually roomy and comfortable.

During breakfast Ma talked to me about integrity, and what it means to make a decision and accept the consequences. It sucks that Dad's not here right now but what's inconvenient or disappointing for me, is actually really important to Dad. I respect that. At least, I'm going to try.

The sudden sound of a horse neighing prompts me to join the conversation. "Are there horses in this park?" I ask.

Clare looks at me over her shoulder and says, "I'm afraid not. Do you like horseback riding? I know of an equestrian camp you could join."

"Qing Yuan loves trying new things," Ma says and the two of them go back to their previous conversation.

I scan the meadow for proof that there *are* horses in the park. But after a while, I give up and accept that my ears must have been playing a trick on me.

I can see the museum up ahead. It looks like a castle set on a hill! I start making a plan in my mind: first we'll visit the tapestry rooms and then we'll look at the illuminated manuscripts. The website said that parts of this museum are built from actual medieval ruins in Europe. Entire chapels were taken apart, stone by stone, and shipped to Washington Heights to be reassembled. I used to want to be an archaeologist but these days I think I want to be a curator. I'd love to be the person who gets to decide what goes on display in a museum.

Mama always reminds me that every continent has its own history—not just Europe. I'm really into castles but last summer I got to climb the steps of two Aztec pyramids when our family went to Mexico. In Teotihuacán, at the end of the Avenue of the Dead, is the Temple of the Moon. There's also a Temple of the Sun. Astronomy was really important to Indigenous people. It's important to everybody, really, because we all live under the same sky. There's a big eclipse coming up next week that will cast a shadow across the entire country for a little while. I haven't got the special glasses you need to watch the moon block the sun, but Ma says we can probably get some at the local library.

I pull the looking drop out of my pocket. All Dad said about it in his letter was that he bought it at a flea market. I guess I'll have to ask Dad about it when he calls tonight. I've already decided not to avoid his calls any more. I really miss him and that's what I'll say.

Going to Mexico with him was one of the best trips ever. Ma was pregnant with Sophie so she stayed home, and Dad met me and Mama in Mexico City. I won't lie—it was cool to look like a regular family for a while. But the best part was having Dad around to teach me about Gaspar Yanga and the community founded by runaway slaves in Veracruz. I never knew there were Black people in Mexico. Mama says in a few more years I can read one of her favorite books, *They Came Before Columbus*. Then I'll know what she likes to call "the real deal."

I'm thinking about the eclipse, and the museum, and my

dad when something strange happens. The looking drop turns to ice! It's so cold that it becomes hard to hold and I nearly drop it on the paved path.

Ma hears me gasp and quickly turns around. "Are you okay?"

Holding something really cold is almost as painful as holding something really hot! I toss the icy mirror from hand to hand and manage to nod at Ma. Then Sophie starts to cry and Ma says maybe we better stop and feed her before going into the museum. There are never any places for Ma to feed Sophie when we're out in public, and breastfeeding is another one of those things that make some people freak out.

Clare points to some nearby picnic tables before saying goodbye. Ma promises to keep in touch and then we walk over to one of the shady tables. While Sophie's having her mid-morning snack, I take a closer look at the round mirror. It's no longer too cold to hold, but I can scrape frost off the glass with my fingernail. Suddenly I hear the sound of a horse galloping toward us. I look up but there aren't even any dogs in the park right now. Then a horse neighs right next to me and I jump in surprise, dropping the mirror on the ground.

The soft grass prevents it from breaking but when I reach down to pick it up, I notice something has changed. Instead of seeing my own reflection staring up at me, I can see *through* the looking drop to the ground beneath it.

Sophie burps and Ma slips the strap of the carrier over her shoulder once more. "Ready to go?" she asks with a smile.

I nod, put the looking drop in my pocket, and head up the hill that leads to the museum's entrance.

3

The museum looks sort of like a castle from the outside even though it's meant to look more like a monastery. There's no moat or drawbridge, but we do pass a portcullis that makes the museum seem fortress-like. Glossy green ivy crawls up the high wall, the paved road changes to cobblestones, and a tower with a red-tiled roof rises above us. I've never been to Europe, but I feel like I've traveled back in time to a world of monks and knights and kings and queens. Two red banners hang down the grey stone wall telling us we have arrived at The Cloisters!

In the middle of the banners is a wide arched doorway. As soon as I step inside, I feel like I'm in a sacred place— like a cathedral. The lobby has a vaulted ceiling, and it's dim and cool compared to the bright sunshine of the park. The museum has only been open for a few minutes, but already there's a steady stream of visitors. We climb a long stone staircase and join the line to buy our tickets. I reach inside my pocket and wrap my hand around the looking drop. It's no longer cold but my fingers tingle just the same. I think something special is going to happen today!

Sophie spots another baby in the arms of the man

standing in line in front of us and next thing you know, Ma's talking to a stranger again. He mentions that his son's first birthday is coming up and Ma tells him that she makes cakes for special occasions (her cakes are amazing, and I'm not just saying that 'cause I'm her son and get to lick out all the bowls). But right now I feel like I'm the only person in this family that can't find a friend! Sophie's patting the chubby cheeks of the other baby and Ma's telling the kid's father about her vegan cakes.

On our tickets is a sticker we peel off and wear as proof of admission. I put mine on my t-shirt and then grab a free map so I can decide where to start our tour. But then Ma pulls out one of her business cards and starts telling the man about sugar-free icing. I interrupt as politely as I can and ask if I can explore the museum on my own.

Ma tries not to look hurt. "I thought we were going to look around together."

I assure Ma I won't go beyond the Late Gothic Hall. She nods and says, "Okay, but stay where I can see you, please."

The first thing I notice when I step into the gallery is a painted wooden statue of a Black man! The nearby plaque on the wall says he's one of the Three Kings and that the statues used to sit on an altar in Germany. He's wearing fancy clothes for the time—a brocade tunic over tights—and he's holding a golden chalice in one hand and its lid in another. Some people say three kings visited Jesus, others say the Magi were actually magicians or astrologers and that's why they knew how to follow the star to Bethlehem.

In the nativity story, Balthazar's gift to the baby was

myrrh. I know that because my grandparents in Texas sent me a book of bible stories for Christmas last year. Mama wanted to send it back, but Ma said I could keep it since it was a gift. When my moms got married, Mama's parents didn't come to the wedding. In the book they wrote, "We'll be praying for you, dear."

I wish Mama were here now. She's not too thrilled about me being into medieval stuff because she thinks I find it more interesting than my own history. But that's not true—there was a lot going on in Asia and Africa during the Middle Ages. I know all about Genghis Khan and Mansa Musa. He ruled most of West Africa in the 1300s and was the richest person who ever lived!

There were also lots of people of color living in Europe during that time, though you wouldn't know it from the art in the museum. I wander around the gallery but other than Balthazar, no one else has skin like mine. Most of the wall art and artifacts in glass cases are what's called "religious iconography"—stuff you'd find in a medieval church. If I was the curator of this museum, I'd put on display art that showed just how diverse the medieval world really was.

When I finish inspecting everything in this gallery, I turn back and look for Ma. She's in front of a weird statue that seems to delight my little sister. Sophie presses her finger to the glass as if the statue of a naked baby Jesus holding an apple were real.

"Ma, I'm going into the next gallery, okay?"

She nods and drifts in the same direction. The next room doesn't have much in it besides some pretty stained glass windows, so I keep on going. There are tapestries in the next gallery that take up the entire wall! One shows a group of people bathing a falcon. Hunting with raptors was a popular sport in the Middle Ages—if you were rich.

Poor people don't usually show up in art because it's the rich people who pay for the paintings, or sculptures, or tapestries and they only want to see themselves. Mama pointed that out to me when we went to a museum in Chicago. That's why she likes folk art—because it's made by everyday people—people who are more like us.

Sometimes I wonder what it would be like to live in the Middle Ages. Dad says I probably wouldn't live long because people didn't understand the connection between hygiene and health. I definitely wouldn't want to catch The Plague, but I could see myself living in a monastery with a bunch of monks. Unlike most people, they could read and write, and they grew herbs in their gardens that could be used to treat some illnesses. I'd be okay taking a vow of poverty and I'd be happy not saying a word to anyone while I painted beautiful illustrations for a bestiary. That's a medieval book about mythical animals.

Sophie's starting to fuss, which means we'll probably have to leave before too long. We haven't even seen all the galleries on the top floor and there are more rooms to see downstairs. I check the map and pick up the pace. When I look up again, I find myself face to face with one of my favorite mythical creatures—a unicorn!

All the walls in this tapestry room are covered with woven pictures, though there's a massive fireplace stretching along one wall. I wander around the small room and find a long tusk from a narwhal standing in the corner. A plaque in front of the tusk says that medieval artists were inspired by the whale's long, spiral tusk and so depicted unicorns with similar horns.

Each tapestry shows a different part of a story. A plaque on the wall says that the seven tapestries together are called *Hunt of the Unicorn*. I slowly walk around the room and wonder if medieval people looked at tapestries the way we watch television. There are lots of dogs and men with spears. The unicorn uses its horn to defend itself but in the end, the hunters win. Once they kill the unicorn, they put its limp, bleeding body over the back of a horse and head back to the city where a crowd has gathered to greet them.

Mama shared her favorite quote with me once. I can't remember exactly how it goes, but it suggests a lion would tell a much different story than the hunter that killed it. I wonder what story the unicorn would tell if it was ever given the chance.

My favorite tapestry in this room is the one with no people at all—just the unicorn resting in a meadow full of flowers. A wooden fence surrounds the unicorn and it wears a strange belt-like collar around its neck. It's chained to a pomegranate tree but the unicorn seems content. I guess it's better to be someone's pet than to be hunted and killed.

I stand in front of the tapestry so long that even Ma and Sophie move on to the next gallery. I think about the sounds I heard in the park and wonder where this majestic, magical creature would go if it weren't chained to the tree.

Maybe I'm a bit blue because of my own friendless state, but I can't help feeling sorry for the lonely unicorn. I even blink away a couple of tears!

Sophie's familiar wail comes from the next gallery so I finally tear myself away from the unicorn tapestry. But just as I turn to go, the looking drop grabs my attention by turning to ice in my pocket. I use the hem of my t-shirt to pull it out without freezing my fingers. Then I rub off the frost and look through the glass. My heart skips a beat when I see a hoof and a slender white leg stepping onto the floor!

Shocked, I fall back and hold up the looking drop so I can see if the tapestry has changed. It seems the same at first, but I look more closely and realize that the woven unicorn is coming undone! As the white thread vanishes, it leaves bare the cords that run from the top to the bottom of the tapestry. But the unicorn clearly doesn't care about the hole it's leaving behind. The animal is determined to be free and easily climbs over the woven fence meant to contain it once the chain at its neck disappears.

When the last loop of white thread disappears from the tapestry, the unicorn stands before me. It neighs triumphantly and proudly tosses its head before bolting from the room. The sound of its hooves galloping through the museum is followed by shrieks as people are knocked down by the invisible unicorn.

Ma hurries back into the room to check on me. "Are you alright, Qing Yuan?"

I nod and slip the looking drop back in my pocket a moment before I feel a hand clamp down on my shoulder.

"Excuse me!" Ma cries with indignation. "Take your hands off my son!"

"This boy was the closest to the tapestry when it was vandalized," the guard insists.

"How dare you accuse my son. Qing Yuan would never do anything to harm such a priceless artifact."

"I wouldn't, I swear!" I cry.

The guard removes his hand but glares at me and says, "I saw you put something in your pocket. What was it— some sort of knife?"

At that point, Ma loses it. She starts yelling at the guard and demanding to see a supervisor. The guard is yelling, too, telling her he has a job to do. Sophie starts bawling and a crowd gathers around us. I pull the looking drop out and hold it up for everyone to see.

"This is it! It's just a mirror." It's much more than a mirror, of course, but I'm not about to tell anyone what the looking drop can do.

"Satisfied?" Ma asks with a glare.

The guard's face turns red. He doesn't know what to say and doesn't even get the chance because a red-haired woman in a grey pantsuit comes over and instructs him to clear the room.

"I'd like to file a formal complaint," Ma says, refusing to budge even though Sophie's crying pitifully.

The woman in the grey suit starts apologizing for what she calls "the misunderstanding."

"It was *not* a misunderstanding," Ma insists. "Your employee saw my child, a Black boy, and automatically

assumed he was a criminal. He's ten years old, for goodness sake! I can assure you that I will be speaking with our attorney as soon as I get home. Until we receive an official apology from the museum—in writing—my family will not step foot in this building again!"

With that, Ma grabs my hand and storms out of the museum. I know better than to interrupt her dramatic exit, but the last thing I want to do right now is go home! I need to explore the rest of the museum. I need to find the phantom unicorn!

4

Ma wasn't kidding—she really does call her lawyer friend as soon as we get home. But that's only after she Face Timed Mama on our way back from the museum. Mama kept asking me if I was okay and I kept assuring her that I was. It sucks being accused of something you didn't do, but it's happened so many times that I'm used to it.

Now Sophie's napping and Ma's on the computer angrily typing an email to the museum's board of trustees. I know I should help her—it did happen to me, after all—but instead I slip out of the apartment and go downstairs. There's a nice garden at the front of our building and all the flowers are in bloom. I perch on a low stone wall next to the hydrangeas and think about what happened at The Cloisters. Not to me, to the unicorn. I have to find a way to get back to the museum! But how can I when Ma's ready to organize a boycott?

"Hey."

I look up and see a blond boy standing in front of me. I glance around just in case this kid isn't talking to me. But I'm the only one around so I say, "Hey."

He sits next to me and smiles. "You're new around here,

23

huh?"

I nod and force my feet not to walk away. Maybe this kid could be my first friend! Or maybe he'll ask me questions I'd rather not answer. If I tell him the truth, he might think I'm weird but if I don't answer at all, he might think I'm a snob. I shove my hands in my pockets. The looking drop feels warm.

"My family moved in last week," I tell him.

"Welcome to the building," the kid says, holding out his hand for me to shake. "I'm Ari. What's your name?"

"Q," I tell him, hoping he'll accept it and move on.

No such luck. Ari tilts his head to one side and asks, "What's the Q stand for? Quincy? Quentin? Quiznos?"

I've never heard of that last one but Ari's smiling so I guess it must be some kind of joke. "You can just call me Q," I say.

"My name sucks, too," Ari says with a sigh.

I smile just a little. "Actually, I really like my name but it confuses people so I just stick with Q." I hesitate and then add, "My full name is Qing Yuan Douglass Jackson-Li."

Ari nods. "That's a mouthful, alright. Does it mean anything special?"

"Qing Yuan mean 'deep water,'" I tell him.

"That's not so bad," Ari says with a shrug. "My name means 'lion of God' but I still get razzed. Ari's short for Ariel," he explains.

I try to smother a smile. "Like in *The Little Mermaid*?"

"Exactly," Ari says while rolling his eyes. "My friends call me Ari, but every year on the first day of school, the teacher calls out my full name and some joker starts singing 'Under the Sea.'"

We both laugh at that. I like talking to Ari. Just as I'm searching for something else to say, the looking drop turns to ice. I wince and quickly pull my hand out of my pocket.

"You okay?" Ari asks.

I nod and reach back into my pocket. I pull out the looking drop by the string so my fingers don't freeze. "My dad sent me this."

Ari peers into the mottled surface of the small round mirror. "What is it?"

"I'm not sure. In his letter he called it a 'looking drop.' It gets really cold sometimes, and then—"

Ari waits for me to finish my sentence but I close my mouth and slip the looking drop back into my pocket.

"What happens next?"

I shrug and look down the block. An ambulance siren wails in the distance but I still hear the clop of galloping hooves on the pavement. Could the unicorn be nearby? I was so close to making a new friend! But if I tell Ari what happened at the museum today, he'll think I'm weird.

When I finally bring my eyes back to Ari's face, he surprises me by saying, "My grandfather used to run an antiques shop. Let's show it to him and see what he thinks."

I nod and follow Ari across the street and up the block. We stop at a little park. Benches are arranged in a semi-circle and old folks with even older dogs are making the most of the shade. Ari leads me over to a bench where an enthusiastic game of checkers is underway. An old man in

a fedora sees us coming and taps his opponent on the arm. A man with frizzy grey hair rising above his ears turns and looks at us over the thick black rim of his glasses.

"Ari!" he cries. To the other old folks he says, "This is my favorite grandson. He's very bright—wants to be an astronaut!"

"Well, he better hurry up and build us a colony on Mars. We need another exodus the way things are going in this country—"

"Hush, Eli," says a plump woman with a flushed red face. She swats him with her paper fan. When her friend does as he's told, she smiles at us and starts fanning herself once more.

Ari's grandfather puts a wrinkled hand on either side of his face and plants a kiss on his forehead. Ari loops his arm around his grandfather's neck and leans into him.

"Need some money?" his grandfather asks.

"No, Zayde. We're here for an appraisal. This is Q," Ari says, nodding at me. Then he whispers, "Show him!"

I pull the looking drop from my pocket and hand it to Ari's grandfather. He slides his glasses farther down his nose and examines the round mirror. To my surprise, he lifts it to his mouth and bites the metal ring. "Hmm. Eighteen carat gold, I'd say. You have a very valuable mirror, my boy."

"It was a gift," I say softly as the kind old man hands me the looking drop.

"What is this, *Antiques Roadshow*? Enough with the tchatchkes! Make your move, Saul."

Ari's grandfather waves his hand at his opponent who

frowns but says nothing more.

"The mirror gets really cold sometimes," Ari tells his grandfather. "Why would it do that, Zayde?"

His grandfather tilts his head from side to side. "Gold is a metal and metal is a conductor. You're a scientist—you know this already."

Ari nods and plants a kiss on his grandfather's cheek. "Thanks, Zayde. See you later."

As we walk away from the old folks, they resume the conversation they halted for our sake. I hear the woman with the fan say, "I never thought I'd see that terrible flag flying in America."

The man she shushed before replies, "It's a new day, Ethel. This country ain't what it used to be."

That makes me think of those red baseball caps that get Mama so upset. I haven't seen any since we moved to New York, but I saw one or two White people wearing them when we went camping last year.

Suddenly I see fingers. Ari's waving his hand in front of my face to get my attention.

"Sorry about that," I say. "I got distracted."

"That's okay. I was just saying that I'll ask my grandfather about your mirror again this evening," Ari tells me. "That's when Zayde likes to tell stories—stories with magic!"

We cross the street and head back to our building. It's been fun having a friend, even just for a few minutes. I watch as Ari pushes open the glass door that leads to the lobby.

"Want to come up to my place?" he asks over his

shoulder.

I sigh with relief and nod eagerly. Ari leads me inside the building and we take the elevator up to the fifth floor. The door to his apartment is unlocked and I can hear men shouting inside. I follow Ari in and he leads me to the kitchen. There are no men but an elderly woman is perched on a stool, her eyes glued to a small television on the counter. Angry White men are marching with torches and waving scary red flags that I've seen in my social studies textbook. People waved those flags when our country was at war a long time ago, but we're not at war any more. Are we?

"Ma—turn that off," says Ari's mother. "The kids don't need to see that crap."

"What a bunch of schmucks," the older woman says with disgust before turning off the television. The flames, red flags, and angry voices disappear.

"We're not babies, Ema," Ari says. "We know what's going on in the world."

I think Ari sounds pretty sophisticated but his mother doesn't look impressed.

"Really? What's going on in your room?" she asks pointedly. "I hope you aren't going to make your new friend play in that pigsty."

"If my room's a mess, it's because of the three little pigs—not me!" Ari insists. Then he turns to the elderly woman and says, "This is my Bubbe. She can't hear too well so you'll have to speak up." As if to demonstrate, Ari loudly announces, "This is Q. His family just moved into the building."

"Do you like rugelach?" Ari's grandmother asks.

Ari nudges me with his elbow. "Just say yes," he advises, so I do.

"Yes, ma'am," I say loudly but respectfully.

She beams at me and says to Ari's mother, "Such nice manners!" Then she takes a tin from the counter and opens it to reveal dozens of homemade cookies. "Take as many as you like," she says with a smile.

Ari knocks my outstretched hand aside and grabs the whole tin. "We'll be in my room if you need us."

But when we get to Ari's room, his three younger brothers—the "three little pigs"—are already there playing. Or fighting. It's hard to tell. Ari yells at them to leave but they just tackle each other and ignore him.

"We could go to my place," I suggest.

"Are you an only child?" Ari asks hopefully.

I shake my head. "Not anymore. I have a baby sister but she sleeps most of the time. I have my own room. Want to see it?"

Ari nods and steps over the tangled bodies of his brothers. "Anything for some peace and quiet," he says.

We stop in the kitchen on our way out. Ari snatches the lid to the cookie tin off the counter and tells his mother he'll be home in time for supper.

"Mind your manners!" she calls after him but Ari's already out the front door.

He waits for me to take the lead and we go up the stairs instead of waiting for the elevator. I pull the key from around my neck and let us into the apartment. I can hear

Mama singing softly to Sophie so I don't call out to let her know I'm home. We go straight to my room but when I open the door, I remember that the castle is lying in pieces on the floor.

"Uh—sorry about the mess," I say. "I had a bit of an accident."

Ari looks at the shattered castle and nods once. For some reason, I decide to tell him the truth.

"It wasn't an accident, really. I got mad and smashed it," I confess.

Ari sits on the edge of my bed and opens the round tin. He lets me take a cookie first and then shoves one in his own mouth. After chewing thoughtfully for a while, Ari swallows and says, "Got anything to drink?"

I head to the kitchen and pour two glasses of juice. When I get back to my room, Ari's kneeling on the floor with two hunks of the castle in his hands. "Most of the castle is still intact," he says. "I can help you fix it, if you want."

I set the glasses on my nightstand before kneeling next to Ari. "It took me a long time to assemble this castle. It's a level 4," I tell him, hoping he'll be impressed. "My dad sent it to me for my birthday."

"Your dad doesn't live with you?" Ari asks while gathering up the smaller pieces.

I press my lips together and wish I hadn't mentioned my dad. Ari's sure to ask lots of questions now. "No. He lives in DC."

Ari nods and keeps picking up the tiny grey blocks that

are scattered across the floor. "Are your folks divorced?"

I just shake my head this time and when Ari turns to look at me I sigh and say, "It's complicated."

"Families always are," he says with a grin.

We work in silence for a while. Something about the way Ari's not asking questions makes me want to tell him more. I clear my throat and say, "My dad was supposed to come visit this week. But then his trip got canceled at the last minute."

"Is that why you smashed the castle?" Ari asks.

I nod and dump two handfuls of Lego pieces onto the table. "I really wanted to see him. I miss him a lot."

Ari doesn't sneer or laugh at me. He just empties his hands as well and starts sorting the pieces by color. "I bet your dad misses you, too. That's why he sent you that funny little mirror."

If I tell Ari what happened at the museum, will he believe me? I pull the "funny little mirror" out of my pocket and offer it to Ari. He sets the blocks down and takes it from me. "What happens when it gets cold?"

I sit down on the edge of my bed and Ari sits next to me. He turns it over in his hands, inspecting the mirrors on both sides.

"Can you keep a secret?" I ask.

Ari nods and hands the looking drop back to me. I take a deep breath and tell him everything that happened in the park and the tapestry room at the museum.

When I finish my strange story, Ari folds his arms across his chest and rolls his lips together. Finally he jumps up and declares, "We have to go back!"

"I want to," I tell him, "but I don't think my mom would let me go after what happened today. Plus she's got Sophie to look after and I think she has a client coming over tomorrow."

"I can get us into the museum," Ari assures me.

"How?" I ask.

"My Uncle David is an archivist at The Cloisters. He lets me in all the time."

"And he'll be working on Sunday?"

Ari nods. "The museum is open seven days a week so my uncle gets to choose his own weekend. He takes Friday and Saturday off to observe Shabbat. If you meet me in front of our building at 9:30, we'll get there just before the museum opens. Cool?"

"Cool!" I say with a big grin.

Ari grins back and we get to work fixing my castle.

5

The next morning I'm so excited that I wake up before everyone else—even Sophie. I get dressed, eat breakfast, and fill my water bottle before putting it in my knapsack. Dad didn't call last night so I sit on my bed and reread his letter. I didn't notice before that it's written on the back of a flyer that says, "STOP THE HATE! JOIN THE MARCH FOR PEACE!"

Dad's handwriting has always been kind of messy, but this letter is even harder to read because he says he's writing it in the back of a police van. I'm not sure how Dad got the letter to Thandie, but I'm glad she mailed it to me along with the looking drop. When I finish reading, one line stays in my mind: "In all that I do, I try to put you first, son." I don't feel like anyone's priority these days, but it helps to know that Dad's thinking of me even though he's far away.

When Ma comes into the kitchen with Sophie, I tell her that Ari and I are going to Fort Tryon Park. Technically that isn't a lie since we have to pass through the park to reach The Cloisters. I take the elevator downstairs and find Ari waiting for me in front of the building.

"Have you got the looking drop?" he asks anxiously.

I nod and pat the pocket of my cargo shorts. Ari looks relieved. "I think your dad sent you something really special. Mirrors can be very powerful, you know."

"Really?"

Ari nods solemnly and my heart swells a bit. I'm proud that my dad thought he could trust me with something so valuable. As we head to the park, Ari shares what his grandfather told him about mirrors.

"A mirror is a piece of glass that's painted on one side so it can reflect light. In the old days, people had to use polished stones or copper or bronze. Then they started coating glass with metal."

"They first made those in China," I tell him. "Ma also said that in ancient times, Chinese people used to wear tiny mirrors on their clothes to ward off evil spirits."

Ari rolls his lips together as if he's savoring my words. Then he says, "In our culture, when someone dies we cover all the mirrors as part of sitting Shiva. When you're grieving, you should focus on what you're feeling inside, not how you look on the outside. Zayde said some Jews believe evil spirits come to your house after someone dies, but Bubbe said that's narishkayt—foolishness.

"Zayde also told me that in some cultures, mirrors are used to reverse evil spells because you can reflect negative energy back onto the person trying to curse you. Bubbe laughed but I think it's kind of cool."

I nod and for a while we just walk along in silence. I don't feel like I *have* to say anything, but I really appreciate

Ari asking his grandparents about my looking drop. Maybe that's why I decide to tell him the truth.

I clear my throat and say, "I told you yesterday that my dad's trip got canceled, but I didn't tell you why." I pull dad's letter out of my back pocket and hand it to Ari. "Dad was supposed to drive up and spend the weekend with us, but I guess he went to this rally instead. Then people started fighting and...my dad got arrested."

Ari stops walking and unfolds the letter. Like me, he has to squint to read what Dad scribbled on the back of the crumpled flyer. Then Ari hands it back to me and says, "Your dad's just like Martin Luther King. When he got arrested for protesting segregation in the South, Dr. King wrote a letter on a newspaper someone smuggled into the jail."

I think about that for a moment. Then I wonder how a kid like Ari knows about what happened in Alabama fifty years ago. My parents have taught me all about the Civil Rights Movement. Maybe Ari learned about it at school during Black History Month.

"How do you know so much about Dr. King?" I ask.

Ari looks at me like I'm nuts. "Are you serious? Martin Luther King is a *legend* in my family. My great-uncle Dov was a rabbi. We have a picture of him shaking hands with Dr. King!"

"Wow—that's so cool!"

Ari nods proudly and says, "It's on the wall in our living room. I'll show you the next time you come over."

Suddenly Ari's green eyes open wide. "Did your dad

punch a Nazi? I'd *totally* punch a Nazi if I had the chance. Superman did—so did Captain America and Wonder Woman. Wow, Q—your dad's a hero!" Ari exclaims.

I never thought of it that way. "I don't think my dad punched anyone. He believes in nonviolence."

Ari tries to hide his disappointment. "Just like Dr. King. Why'd your dad get arrested if he didn't punch anyone?"

I shrug and put Dad's letter back in my pocket. I don't tell Ari that I haven't wanted to talk to my dad since his arrest. I silently sigh with relief when Ari chuckles and talks about his family instead of mine.

"My aunt protests *everything!*" he says. "Fracking, Wall Street, police brutality. Bubbe makes a big fuss every time Aunt Mimi goes to a rally, but deep down I can tell she's proud of my aunt. It takes guts to stand up for what you believe."

We start walking again and I point to the spot in the park where I heard something galloping across the meadow.

"You're sure it wasn't a horse?" Ari asks, scanning the ground for hoof prints.

"I didn't see anything, but I heard it neigh—twice!"

Ari thinks for a moment. "What do you know about unicorns?" he asks.

"Not much," I admit. "I checked some of the books I have, but they only said that unicorns are super fast and their horns make you immune to poison. Oh—and they're mentioned in the Bible a few times."

Ari smiles. "My Uncle David told me that's just because the Greeks made a mistake when they were translating the

Old Testament. Our holy books are written in Hebrew. One book described a type of ox the Greeks had never seen before and so they translated it as 'monoceros.'"

"Sounds like rhinoceros," I say.

"Folks in the Middle Ages called those unicorns, too! But there aren't any rhinoceros tapestries at The Cloisters. It sounds like your looking drop turns to ice whenever the unicorn is nearby. Maybe you should keep it out so you can see when it's frosting over," Ari suggests.

"Good idea."

I pull my house key out of my t-shirt and untie the knotted leather cord. Then I slip the key in my pocket and slide the cord through the metal loop so that the looking drop hangs from my neck.

"If I see it start to frost over, I'll let you know," Ari says.

I nod and head up the hill that leads to the museum entrance. Ari tugs my arm.

"This way," he says. "My uncle's going to meet us at the staff entrance."

Ari pulls out a flip phone and makes a call. "Hi, Uncle David. We're here," he says.

By the time we reach the door, Ari's uncle is waiting there for us. He shakes my hand when Ari introduces us but seems kind of anxious.

"Here you go," Uncle David says, handing each of us a white admission sticker. "Make sure it's visible, otherwise the guards will wonder how you got in."

I thank him and put my sticker on my shirt. We definitely don't want to attract the attention of the museum's security guards. There's one in each gallery but if the museum is as busy as it was yesterday, Ari and I shouldn't have any trouble blending in with the tourists.

"I hope you boys weren't hoping to visit the unicorn tapestry room," Uncle David says. "I'm afraid it's closed today and will be off limits indefinitely until they figure out what happened in there yesterday."

Ari and I exchange glances. "What happened, Uncle David?" he asks innocently.

"It's hard to say, really. Only one tapestry seems to have been vandalized, but it's hard to imagine how anyone could do so much damage without being seen."

Ari winks at me and I smother a grin. It feels good having a secret to share with my new friend. I jump when Uncle David changes the subject suddenly.

"That's a very interesting necklace you've got there, Q."

I pick up the looking glass and hold it out to him. "It's not a necklace, really. It's a looking drop," I tell him.

Uncle David bends down to inspect the round mirror.

"Zayde says it's 18-carat gold," Ari tells him.

"I think Zayde's right," Uncle David replies. He turns the mirror and then rubs his thumb along the gold rim. "Moorish, I'd say, judging from the Arabic inscription."

Ari grabs the looking drop out of his uncle's hand. "Inscription? We didn't see an inscription."

Ari examines the mirror before handing it back to me. "He's right—look!"

I check the mirror's rim. I thought the faint markings were just decorative, but now I can see that they're script—

words written in a language that I can't read.

"I could have my colleague Dr. Khan translate it for you, if you want to leave it with me," Uncle David offers.

"Uh—that's really nice of you, but…" I look at Ari to see what he thinks we should do.

"Maybe later," he tells his uncle. "We're kind of in a rush right now. Thanks for letting us in, Uncle David." Ari grabs my arm and pulls me away.

"Stay out of trouble, Ariel," his uncle calls after us.

Ari grins and waves at his uncle. I glance over my shoulder and watch as he heads back to his office.

"Can I ask you a question?"

"Sure," Ari says.

"How come you don't wear that little hat on your head like your uncle does?"

"You mean a yarmulke? I do wear one when I go to temple," Ari explains. "Uncle David wears his everyday because he's Orthodox. You probably saw his tzitzit, too—those white strings dangling from his shirt? I wear this."

Ari pulls a delicate gold star from under his collar. I didn't notice that he was wearing a necklace.

"It's the Star of David," he tells me. "There are lots of different ways to be Jewish—my family's proof of that! We don't all dress the same, or eat the same foods, or follow the same rules. Like you said before, it's complicated!"

We quiet our laughter as we enter the Late Gothic Hall. After we pass the weird naked baby holding an apple, Ari says, "Don't walk too fast. We've got to blend in, remember?"

I nod and pretend to consider my map even though I know we're heading straight for the tapestry room. But we stop short when we see a security guard standing beneath the ornately carved marble doorway. It's not the same one from yesterday, which is good, but I can see another guard standing in the other doorway on the far side of the room. That means there's no way in.

A stand bearing a sign has been positioned next to the female guard: "EXHIBIT CLOSED UNTIL FURTHER NOTICE." She has her hands clasped behind her back and a stern look on her face. When she starts giving us the evil eye, Ari and I walk over to a nearby altar and pretend to look at it instead.

"What's the plan?" I whisper. I look at Ari, waiting for him to answer, but he's not looking at me. His eyes are fixed on the looking drop.

"Do you feel that?" he asks.

Now that he's mentioned it, I do feel a cool pressure against my chest. I pick up the mirror. It's cold to touch but the glass hasn't frosted over like before.

"What's happening?" I ask anxiously.

"I don't know," Ari replies, "but we need to get inside that room."

I'm about to agree when I see something that makes my mouth fall open.

"What's wrong?" Ari asks.

I try to answer but shock steals my words. Ari spins and tries to see past the guard blocking the door. Within seconds,

his mouth is just as round as mine. In the far corner of the room, next to the narwhal tusk, a boy is climbing out of the tapestry!

6

The guard is so busy watching us that she doesn't notice what's happening behind her in the tapestry room.

I turn my back to the guard but keep talking to Ari. "Do you see him?"

Ari closes his mouth and tries to act normal but I hear the astonishment in his voice. "I can't believe it! He's—he's unraveling himself! I mean, there's a real boy standing in the corner. But on the tapestry there's a gap where the boy used to be."

I really want to turn around and look but force myself to face the altar instead. "That's just what the unicorn did yesterday," I tell Ari. "But once the thread came out, the unicorn disappeared. I wonder why we can still see that boy. What's he doing now?" I ask Ari.

"He's creeping along the wall—I think he's going over to the damaged tapestry," Ari says. "If we can see him, the guards can see him, too. He's got to be careful. Tell him to hide!"

I finally turn around but pretend to admire the stone curlicues carved into the arched doorway above the guard's head. "How do I do that?" I ask Ari. "Does he even speak

English? The tapestries were made in Brussels, you know. Maybe he speaks French or German—or Flemish!"

"Just give him a sign," Ari suggests. "I'll go distract the guard."

Ari walks over, opens his map, and pretends to ask the guard for directions. I discreetly wave my hand over my head until I get the boy's attention. Then I point at the guard and shake my head. The boy frowns at me, but when I crouch down close to the stone floor, he does the same.

When I'm sure the boy understands he'll have to sneak past the guard, I move away from the door. Ari's acting as if he doesn't understand English. Frustrated, the guard tries speaking to him in Spanish but Ari still acts perplexed. It's a brilliant tactic because the guard is completely distracted. I watch breathlessly as the boy from the tapestry presses himself flat against the doorway and slips out of the room and into the crowded gallery without the guard noticing. I wave him over and we stand in awkward silence by the falcon tapestry.

While waiting for Ari to join us, I take a closer look at the boy. He's wearing a pink tunic covered with gold swirls. Beneath a braided gold belt, the pleated half of the tunic hangs over wine-colored tights. The soft leather boots on his feet are the same as the ones worn by the Balthazar statue. On his head rests a boxy black wool hat with a silver brooch at the front. I don't know a whole lot about medieval clothes, but I'm guessing this boy is rich—or comes from a rich household. He was holding a dog in the tapestry so maybe he works for a baron or a duke.

"Toda raba," Ari calls to guard before walking away with a wave and a smile.

"What language is that?" I ask when he reaches us.

"Hebrew," Ari replies.

We both look at the finely dressed boy, unsure what to say and in which language. To our surprise, he grasps our hands and speaks first.

"Dank uwel," the boy says with a sincere smile.

For a moment, Ari and I aren't sure how to respond. The confused look on our faces makes the boy laugh. "Forgive me, I will speak your tongue since you clearly don't speak Flemish. I have been learning to speak English for…eighty years! Ever since the tapestries were moved here from France."

Our shock makes the boy laugh again. "Thank you for helping me," he says.

"You're welcome," Ari replies.

The boy pulls the wool hat off his head and shakes out his copper-colored, chin-length hair. "At last! I've had to wear this horrid, itchy hat for centuries. Dressing as a scout was a necessary disguise," he confides.

"Disguise?"

Ari leans in, intrigued. "Are you hiding from someone?"

The boy shudders and glances around nervously. "Yes! Burrgraaf Ector. I couldn't risk being recognized by him, and maids are not permitted to attend the hunt. So I concealed myself by cutting my hair and dressing like a scout."

"You're a maid?" I ask.

He—*she*—nods and glances at her clothes. Her tunic

looks like a girl's dress, but it's actually what men and boys wore in the Middle Ages.

"I'm Gisla," she says with a quick curtsy.

"I'm Qing," I tell her, wondering if I should bow. "And this is Ariel."

Gisla peers into my face. Just when I think she's going to blurt out, "What *are* you?" she declares with total confidence, "You're an Ethiop!"

My mouth falls open but no sound comes out. It's Ari who says, "A *what?*"

"An Ethiop," Gisla repeats.

She's so excited that I almost hate to tell her the truth. "Whoa—hold on there, Gisla. I'm not from Ethiopia."

Gisla frowns and looks at me a doubtfully. "Are you a Moor then? You must be. How else could the Moor's Eye be in your possession?"

I don't know what this girl's talking about but Ari's piecing it together. He points at my chest and then I make the connection, too.

"You mean my looking drop?" I ask, holding it out to her.

Gisla nods without saying a word but the awe in her eyes tells me she's impressed. To my surprise, she falls to her knees in front of me. She reaches for the slowly spinning mirror but dares not touch it.

"Ahhh—at last! I've heard much of this priceless tool. Only five were made and gifted to the most powerful and trusted magi."

I glance at the looking drop and for just a moment

wonder if someone like Balthazar once held it in his hands. Then Gisla jumps up and grabs hold of my arm, jolting me out of my dream.

"Wherever you're from and whoever you are doesn't really matter. You're here now, you've got the Moor's Eye, and you must help me stop Ector before he destroys the last unicorn!"

Gisla's getting excited and a little loud, too. The guard clears her throat and glares at us as a warning.

"Let's go out on the terrace," Ari suggests.

Gisla and I follow him as he leads us out to the Cuxa Cloister. We follow the covered walkway around the quadrangle—a sunny square garden with a trickling fountain in the center. Around it are fruit trees and flowers that would have been grown in a medieval monastery or convent.

We cut through a shadowy room with massive stone arches and go down some steps until we come to a small door at the end of a dimly lit tunnel. A beautiful vertical stained glass window lets in just enough light for me to read the sign on the wooden door: "Exit to West Terrace. Please push."

Ari grasps the black iron ring that serves as a doorknob and does as the sign instructs, but the door doesn't budge. Gisla pushes her shoulder against the door, too, and then it creaks open.

I follow them out onto a stone terrace and breathe a sigh of relief. Through the trees I can see a grey suspension bridge that makes me think of the orange Golden Gate Bridge back home in California. Across the river there are homes dotting the cliffs of what must be New Jersey. I remind myself that I'm in the twenty-first century and *not* the Middle Ages. Somehow the prospect of stopping a unicorn-killer named Ector doesn't seem as daunting in the bright summer sunshine.

"Okay," Ari says. "It's safe to talk out here. Please, tell us everything."

Gisla sighs. "I'm not sure where to begin!"

"Who's Ector?" I ask.

Before she can answer, Ari follows up with a question of his own. "And why is he trying to kill a unicorn?"

Gisla shakes her head sadly. "Not *a* unicorn—*the* unicorn. There's only one left in the world! Laurentia, my mistress, summoned the brightest star in the night sky to guide the poor creature to the shadowlands where it would be safe. But Ector—the cruelest, most vile man in all of Brussels—raised a dense forest and the unicorn was waylaid."

"He *raised* a forest?" Ari says skeptically. "How could he do that?"

Gisla shivers though it's warm on the sunny terrace. "Ector is one of the most powerful wizards to ever live. But he uses his magic to seize whatever he desires from others—not to help and to heal, like my mistress Laurentia. She knew Ector wanted the last unicorn for himself and so she saved it by creating an enchantment. Most people knew Laurentia as a gifted weaver, but she was also a heks—what you would call a witch. She wove the unicorn's essence into the tapestry and wrapped it in a protective spell."

Gisla suddenly turns away and looks out over the river.

We can still see the tears streaming down her cheeks but we don't say anything.

Gisla sniffles so I take a packet of tissues out of my book bag. But when I offer it to her, she doesn't know what to do. I show her how to open the packet and pull out a tissue so she can blow her nose.

After taking a deep breath, Gisla continues telling us her story. "When Ector learned what Laurentia had done, he was furious. So he poisoned my dear, sweet mistress. But with her dying breath, Laurentia cast one final spell and trapped Ector in a tapestry of his own design."

"The Hunt of the Unicorn," I whisper.

Gisla hears me and nods solemnly. Ari and I exchange glances. It's a lot to take in.

"You stepped out of the tapestry, too," I dare to mention. "Did Laurentia cast a spell on you?"

"Oh, no," cries Gisla. "She would never do that! But I was her apprentice, you see. I could only cast simple spells at the time, but when Ector killed my mistress, I vowed I would see her will done. I read every book of spells I could find in her library. Then I repeated the words she used to trap Ector…"

Ari looks at the girl, amazed. "You cursed yourself? Why?"

Gisla sighs with obvious exasperation. "All the while Ector was ensnared in Laurentia's trap, he never stopped scheming and yearning for the unicorn. The tapestries don't tell the entire story. The unicorn was never going to be presented to the king. Once it was killed, Ector planned to open a door that has remained locked for thousands of years."

"What's behind the door?" Ari asks.

Gisla starts pacing the terrace, wringing her hands. I'm not sure she even heard Ari because instead of answering his question, she starts talking about Ector again.

"Ector is heartless! You can see him lurking in the top corner of the tapestry, egging the others on. Just as he whispered bloody commands in the hunters' ears, so he deceived the poor unicorn with false promises of freedom. He cast a spell that allowed the desperate creature to move as a shadow through the museum and into the park beyond. But only for one hour every day—just enough to give the unicorn a taste of freedom. Then, knowing he had the advantage, Ector struck a bargain with the unhappy beast: release from the tapestry in exchange for three drops of blood."

"What can Ector do with three drops of unicorn's blood?" I ask, hoping Gisla won't ignore me, too.

She shudders and stands still. "He won't stop with three. Once he has the unicorn subdued and the knife in his hand, Ector will kill the sacred creature and seize its horn."

"Right—you told us that part already," Ari says impatiently. "You also said Ector was trying to open a door. Why is that such a big deal?"

Once again, Gisla refuses to answer Ari's question. She

clasps her hands together and drops to her knees before me.

"We've got to find Ector and the unicorn. They're shadows—invisible to all. Except the one who holds the Eye."

I take Gisla's arm and help her stand up. "We're going to help you—you don't have to beg."

"Oh, thank you! You're very brave even if you're not a king. But you should know that Ector is extremely dangerous—not only to the unicorn, but to you as well. You have something precious and very powerful in your possession. He will try to claim it for himself."

I feel a bit queasy all of a sudden, but Ari just scoffs at Gisla's warning. "Ha! Let him try."

Gisla stares at Ari for a moment. She can't tell whether he's a fool or incredibly brave. I'm not sure either! I'm happy to help Gisla track down the unicorn but I'd rather not come face to face with this Ector!

I swallow hard and try to do the right thing. "Should we split up or search together?" I ask.

"You have the Eye. If the two of you search for the unicorn, I will consult the sacred texts and see if I can uncover Ector's plan."

"Sacred texts? Where are those?" I ask, looking at my museum map.

"Downstairs," Ari says with confidence. "The illuminated

manuscripts are in the Treasury."

Gisla studies the map for a moment and then heads for the door that leads back inside the museum. "I need to consult the tapestries once more. Meet me in the Treasury in one hour."

When Gisla puts her hat back on her head, Ari says, "Uh—I'd ditch that if I were you. It kind of makes you stand out and right now you really need to fit in."

Gisla shrugs and shoves the black hat behind some potted plants. Then she tugs the iron ring on the heavy wooden door and slips inside.

Ari looks at me. "So—what's the plan?"

"Why are you asking me?"

"Because you've got the Moor's Eye," he replies.

I think for a moment. "The looking drop—or the Eye—should frost over if the unicorn is nearby. But we can also hear its hooves on the stone floors. Where would a unicorn go? Back to the park? Maybe we should stand by the exit," I suggest.

Ari puts a hand on his stomach. "I don't know about you, but I'm kind of hungry. Maybe the unicorn's hungry, too. There's a café downstairs."

"It can't exactly order a sandwich," I remind him.

"No, but there's another cloister next to the café. And in the cloister garden there are pear trees, and pomegranates, and lots of green leafy things that a unicorn might like to eat."

I grin at Ari and say, "Let's go!"

7

We leave the terrace and go back inside the museum.

"Let's take the stairs in the Early Gothic Hall," Ari suggests.

I follow him back inside the museum and we go down a flight of stairs that leads to a chapel with a high vaulted ceiling. Several tomb effigies rest peacefully beneath the tall stained glass windows. I'd like to stop and examine the stone figures, but right now we have a job to do. Gisla wouldn't tell us about the door Ector wants to open, but I have a feeling whatever's behind it should stay locked away for another thousand years!

We leave the chapel and push open the heavy wooden door that leads us back outside. This cloister only has two covered walkways. The other two sides of the quadrangle are bordered by low stone walls that overlook the park below. We step out of the shade and enter the sunny garden. Above us the August sun burns bright in the cloudless blue sky.

The four trees in the garden aren't very tall. It would be easy for a unicorn to nibble at the pears dangling from the low branches. This cloister has a well instead of a fountain but it's covered so the unicorn couldn't get a drink of water here.

"See any signs of the unicorn?" Ari asks quietly. There are a few people looking around the garden, though most are enjoying the shade of the covered walkways.

I shake my head. The looking drop hasn't changed temperature and only the breeze ruffles the leaves on the pear trees. I look down and see a small green sign letting visitors know that the plants in this section of the garden are poisonous. I don't think unicorns can read, so I hope it knows better than to nibble on those particular plants.

Ari and I crisscross the garden until we're sure we haven't missed any sign of the phantom unicorn. Then Ari puts a hand on his stomach and says, "I'm hungry. Let's check the Trie Cloister. It's right next door and I want to get a snack from the café."

We follow the covered walkway into the next room. On a counter in the far corner is rack displaying an assortment of cookies, cake slices, and other treats. People are seated at shaded tables that ring the sunny square garden. In the center is a stone cross that doubles as a fountain.

"Uh oh," Ari says. "Be cool."

Before I can ask him why, his uncle waves at us from a nearby table. A woman with short black hair and bright green glasses is sitting at the table, too. She smiles and takes a sip of her coffee. I try to smile back but I can see her brown eyes fixing on the looking drop. I instinctively wrap my hand around it. It's not cold so that probably means the unicorn isn't here.

"Hello, boys. Keeping out of trouble?" Uncle David asks.

Ari tries to laugh but it comes out sounding more like a wheeze. He gives me a nervous glance and says, "Of course! How can anyone get in trouble at a museum?"

I want to remind him of the security guard who tried to get me in trouble yesterday, but figure it's probably best to keep that story to myself right now.

Uncle David stands up and begins clearing the table. "Well, with the eclipse on Monday and the...perplexing condition of the unicorn tapestry, there's a lot of nervous energy around here today."

"Indeed," says the woman with the funky glasses. She picks up her coffee cup and stands next to Ari's uncle.

"This is my colleague Dr. Samira Khan," he says. "She's a curator here at the museum. We're just finishing up our break. Can I get you boys anything from the café?"

Ari nods eagerly and follows his uncle over to the counter in the corner. I stand awkwardly in front of Dr. Khan. She takes another sip of coffee, keeping her eyes locked on the looking drop resting against my chest. It would be rude to cover it with my hand again, so instead I stare at the stone cross in the center of the quadrangle. Water pours out of several small copper pipes, and I watch as a sparrow positions itself upside down on one pipe in order to get a drink. I smile at the clever little bird and when I look up, Dr. Khan is smiling at me.

"Dr. Lieberman told me you had a Moorish mirror. They are very rare, even for someone in my line of work."

"What do you do here at the museum?" I ask, partly because I'm interested and partly because I want to talk about anything other than my mirror.

"I'm a curator," Dr. Khan says.

"I might be a curator when I grow up," I tell her. "Do you like your job?"

"Very much," Dr. Khan says. "I'm working on a special exhibit right now. It won't open to the public for another year, but it will introduce our visitors to the many contributions of the Moors. Have you heard of them?"

"Sure," I say. "They're Muslims who left north Africa and crossed into Spain."

Dr. Khan nods. "The Moors ruled much of Spain and Portugal for over seven hundred years. They brought to medieval Europe their advanced knowledge of astronomy, mathematics, medicine, and architecture."

"Like the Alhambra!" I cry. "I watched a documentary with my dad about that castle. Well, it's more of a palace, really, with its beautiful gardens and fountains. My dad said he'd look for a model for me to assemble, but I'd like to see the Alhambra for myself someday."

"Then you'll have to visit Grenada," Dr. Khan says. "And I hope you and your father will come see my exhibit when it opens next year. Many people have heard about the Crusades but few know that Muslims, Jews, and Christians once lived together peacefully in the Moorish kingdom of Al-Andalus. Muslims were expelled from Spain in the seventeenth century, but their legacy remains. To this day, thousands of words in the Spanish language are actually

Arabic in origin. The Moors even brought paper to Europe."

"I thought paper came from China," I say. That's what Ma told me.

"It did," Dr. Khan confirms, "but Muslims traveled widely and they brought new inventions with them as they moved from place to place. The Moors changed the culture of Europe for the better, which is what immigrants everywhere do."

Dr. Khan pauses and her gaze drifts down to my looking drop once more. "The Moors were also skilled at making mirrors—much like the one you wear around your neck. May I see it?" she asks politely.

I wrap my hand around the looking drop and think for a moment. Dr. Khan knows a lot more than I do about medieval mirrors, and Ari's uncle did say she could translate the inscription for me. So I pull the leather cord over my head and hand the mirror to Dr. Khan.

She steps into the sunny garden to study the inscription for a moment. Then she comes back over to me and reads it aloud.

اَلْمُؤْمِنْ مِرْآةُ الْمُؤْمِنِ

Her voice sounds like music! I wonder if Dr. Khan could teach me to read the lacy writing, too.

"What does that mean?" I ask.

"It is one of the hadith, an account of the words or actions of the Prophet Muhammad. This hadith means 'A Believer is the mirror for a Believer.'"

I try to come up with my own translation. "So…we see what we want to see?"

Dr. Khan smiles and gives the looking drop back to me. "That's one interpretation. If you have a pure heart, then you will see goodness in others. But if your heart is not pure, you will find fault in others. The mirror shows us our reflection but also our conscience. The inscription could also mean that we should try to be our best selves so that we may serve as an example for others."

"My parents are good role models," I tell Dr. Khan. "I try to be like them and do the right thing, but sometimes it's hard."

Dr. Khan nods sympathetically and says, "Indeed, it is. It takes courage to stand up for what you believe. Fortunately, role models may be found in our families and in our communities. May I give you a piece of advice, young man?"

"Sure," I say. "I could use some right about now."

Dr. Khan smiles again. Then she puts her hand on my shoulder and looks into my eyes. "Remember that the mirror shows us not only what is real, but what is possible."

Before I can think of what to say in return, Ari and his uncle come back. Ari hands me half a slice of pound cake and we wave goodbye to the adults as they head back to work.

We eat our snack as quickly as we can and then head to the Treasury to meet Gisla. As soon as Ari pulls open the glass doors, she rushes over to us and breathlessly exclaims, "I found it! Come with me."

We follow Gisla through the dimly lit room with its maze of glass cases. We pass a selection of prayer books, several reliquaries, and fancy gold jewelry and robes once worn by medieval bishops. Gisla leads us over to the far wall and stops in front of a display case that holds a framed page taken from an illuminated manuscript.

"This is it!" she cries. "This is Ector's plan—I'm sure of it!"

Ari and I take a moment to study the colorfully painted page. Weird black and white striped creatures lie next to several humans, and above them an angel blowing a curved horn floats among the stars. At the bottom of the painting, a man with a key sits in some sort of pit and flames rise up from the hole in the ground, reaching all the way up to the sun.

I can't really tell what's going on so I read the description, too. It doesn't make a whole lot of sense to me, but a few words stand out: stinging scorpions, menacing locusts, and the undead!

"Is this from a medieval bestiary?" I ask.

"I think it's the Book of Revelation," says Ari. "This is a picture of what some monk in Spain thought the apocalypse would look like."

My eyes open wide. "Apocalypse? You mean—"

"The end of the world," Ari says grimly.

Gisla nods solemnly. "The sun will be swallowed and darkness will cover the land. And then—"

Ari and I stare at Gisla, waiting for her to finish her sentence. But her eyes remain glued to the bizarre painting.

Finally, in a voice so soft we have to strain to hear her, Gisla whispers, "Only while the sun is obscured can the gate can be opened."

I take a deep breath. "What's behind the gate?" I ask.

Gisla closes her eyes and shudders. "Demons, evil spirits, and vicious beasts. If unleashed, they will turn your world into a never-ending nightmare."

My stomach twists and I wish I hadn't scarfed down that pound cake. "This is bad," I say.

Ari swallows hard and nods his head in agreement. "This is *really* bad!"

Gisla finally turns away from the terrible painting and faces us instead. "There's something else you should know," she says. "When I went back to the tapestry room, Ector wasn't there."

Ari gasps and unleashes a string of questions. "Wasn't there? Does that mean he's real again? Flesh, not thread? Like, 3D?"

Gisla doesn't know what that means so I explain. "He means three-dimensional—not flat. You're saying Ector's human now, like us?"

"I'm afraid so," Gisla says.

"Can we see him the way we can see you, or is he a phantom like the unicorn?"

"I suspect that Ector's shadow has roamed these halls unseen for years, studying the sacred texts. Now, in order to fulfill his mission, he has returned to his body. Ector is small in stature but I fear his power has grown over time."

"Why has he come back to life now?" I ask.

"The eclipse!" cries Ari. "The moon will pass in front of the sun on Monday."

Gisla nods. "Magic performed in the shadow of the sun is even more dangerous."

"We have to stop Ector," Ari says, but his voice lacks confidence and his face has gone very pale.

Gisla stares at the page in the display case. She's trying to be brave, but I can tell she's scared, too.

I grasp my looking drop and wish my parents were here to tell me what to do. "Maybe we should tell your uncle," I suggest. "Maybe he and Dr. Khan would know what to do."

Ari considers the idea but then shakes his head. "By the time we got them to believe us, it might be too late."

For a moment the three of us stand together in silence. We all know what needs to be done, but none of us is sure we can do it on our own. We're just kids, after all.

Gisla turns so that the painting is behind her. With downcast eyes she admits, "I am only a witch's apprentice— and my training is incomplete."

Then she lifts her chin and looks us in the eye. "But I will use whatever gifts I possess to stop Ector from ruining your world, just as my mistress tried to stop him from ruining ours."

I take Gisla's hand in mine and reach for Ari's. He folds my hand in his and squeezes hard.

"We'll do our part, too. I have the Moor's Eye, and Ari knows this museum like the back of his hand. Right?"

Ari gives us a reassuring nod and Gisla's eyes brighten.

"In a way," she says, "we represent what Ector fears

most."

"He's afraid of three unsupervised kids?" Ari asks doubtfully.

The sound of Gisla's laughter makes all of us feel a bit better. She squeezes our hands and says, "Not likely. But Ector does not like to be challenged by those he feels are beneath him. For us—three children, three *friends*—to unite...for us to risk our lives to preserve the world he wishes to destroy..." Gisla's smile disappears. With a grim face she warns, "Ector's rage will be extreme."

Ari tries to scoff at Gisla's warning but I can tell he's anxious by the way he asks, "What's the worst he can do?"

Before Gisla can answer, I feel my looking drop turn cold.

"Is the unicorn here?" I ask.

"Maybe it's Ector," Ari says in a shaky voice.

We look around us and are shocked to see other visitors fainting. Gisla gasps and points at the floor. A purple mist is snaking through the Treasury, weaving between the display cases and knocking out every person in its path.

"Run!" Gisla cries.

8

We flee from the Treasury and find more people sprawled across the floor of the adjacent gallery. I pull my t-shirt up to cover my mouth. Ari has his arm over his mouth and nose, and Gisla's got both her hands cupped over her face.

"Outside—hurry!" Ari mumbles through his sleeve.

Gisla and I follow him out a dark wooden door that leads back to the two-sided cloister. A few people lie on the stone floor of the covered walkway. We step over them and rush to the far wall. While sucking in several lungfuls of fresh air, I glance at the poisonous plants growing in the garden. I turn to Gisla.

"What's in that mist—some type of poison?"

"It came from Ector, didn't it?" Ari asks anxiously. "He's killed everyone in the museum!"

I think of Ari's uncle and put my arm around his shoulder.

"They're not dead," Gisla assures us. "Ector spread that vapor to put everyone to sleep. He must be planning to use one of the galleries for his ritual. He wouldn't want any witnesses getting in his way."

"Which gallery would he choose?" I ask, pulling out my

map.

"He'll need someplace spacious," Gisla says. "The Treasury is too dark and there isn't enough room for the unicorn to lie down."

"Why don't we check the chapels?" Ari suggests. "The Gothic Chapel is right next door and the two upstairs chapels have even more room."

Before we can decide which one to check first, we hear loud neighing that could only come from an animal in distress.

"The unicorn!" Gisla cries.

"This way," says Ari.

We follow him back inside the museum. The purple mist has evaporated but we have to crawl over a man who collapsed on the stairs leading up to the Gothic Chapel. His loud snoring allows us to creep into the chapel unnoticed.

We stand together, speechless, as we take in the startling scene. At the front of the room, standing in a pool of light, is the unicorn. A short man in medieval clothes is trying to subdue the beautiful beast by tugging at the chain attached to the collar around its neck. My looking drop is cold but I don't need to look through its lens to the see the unicorn— or Ector. It towers over the ugly little man but as he mutters words I can't understand, the unicorn grows quiet and still. Within seconds, the creature folds its legs and settles on the chapel's stone floor, looking as peaceful as it did in the tapestry. But there is no fence to protect the unicorn now.

Ector stands over it with a hideous grin on his face. It's only when he turns to reach for a silver dagger that he sees the three of us at the back of the chapel. His mouth twists as if he has swallowed something sour.

"I will give you one chance and one chance only," he warns. "Leave now or you will share this creature's fate."

"You cannot kill the unicorn—it is a sacred beast!" Gisla cries.

Ector's pale grey eyes narrow as he stares at her. "I know you," he says with a scowl. "You served that witch Laurentia!"

"I did and did so with pride," Gisla declares. "She was the best mistress I ever could have hoped for—and you killed her!"

Ector's laugh makes me shudder. He sounds like a deranged hyena.

"That is what happens to those who dare to thwart my plans. You have been warned!"

Ector's menacing gaze shifts from Gisla to Ari and me. With obvious disdain, his pale eyes sweep over us from head to toe. "Do you really think you can stop me?"

Ari takes a step forward. "Not really," he says with a casual shrug. "But Gisla told us you were the greatest wizard who ever lived and…we wanted to see for ourselves. Right, Q?"

When Ari winks at me, I follow his lead and take a step forward as well. We can't stall Ector forever, but we didn't have time to come up with a plan so stalling will have to do.

"I didn't even believe in magic until I saw the unicorn free itself from the tapestry," I say, trying to sound impressed. "That was amazing! You made that happen, didn't you?"

Still holding the dagger in his hand, Ector moves toward us. The gold thread in his fancy brown brocade tunic glints in the light pouring through the tall stained glass windows. His stringy brown hair is partly covered by a plush blue velvet hat. Ector certainly isn't handsome, but he carries himself like a man who's accustomed to getting what he wants.

"Laurentia trapped the essence of the creature inside the tapestry. I merely offered the unicorn a chance to be free once more. For one hour each day it could roam the ground—but only as a shadow of its former self. To be flesh and blood once more it had to pay a price."

Gisla's cheeks are red and her fists are clenched. "Laurentia only cast that spell to protect the unicorn from you and your murderous scheme!"

"And I merely reversed her spell in order to fulfill my destiny." Ector glances over his shoulder at the sleeping animal. "We struck a bargain and now it is time for me to collect what I am due."

"The unicorn belongs in the Shadowlands," Gisla insists with a stamp of her foot.

"The unicorn belongs to ME!"

Ector's angry voice echoes through the chapel like thunder. We all cringe but Ari somehow finds the courage to take another step forward.

"We don't doubt your power, sir. But can you tell us why you want to kill the unicorn?"

Ector clearly thinks we're beneath him but he can't resist sharing his plan. "I need its properties—both blood and horn—to create a compound that will produce the purest gold. Only a key made from such gold can open the Devil's Gate."

"That sounds like alchemy," I say.

Ector studies me for a moment. His eyes seem to see right through me and I remind myself not to show too much intelligence. We want to trick him into thinking we're just a bunch of dumb kids.

After a moment, Ector's gaze shifts from my face to the looking drop. He catches a glimpse of his own reflection in the mirror and seems to wince before hastily looking away. After taking a moment to compose himself, Ector arrogantly says, "I see you have brought me a gift."

I pick up the looking drop. "This old thing? It's just a piece of junk my dad bought at a flea market."

Ector frowns. "That is the Moor's Eye. It is priceless and powerful—too powerful to be in the hands of a boy like you. Give it to me."

A boy like me? I want to say something just as hurtful, but instead I heft the mirror in my hand as if to weigh its value. "You seem to like bargains, Ector. Why don't we strike one right now? I'll give you the mirror if you give me that cool dagger," I propose.

Beside me Gisla gasps. "You mustn't," she whispers but Ari gives me a nod of approval.

"That sounds fair to me," he says. "What do you say, Ector? That's an awfully fancy knife you got there. And we'd love to have a souvenir from our trip to the museum."

Ector turns over the dagger in his hand. The jewels in its

hilt sparkle in the sunlight streaming through the windows.

Finally he looks at me and says, "I do not bargain with children or fools. Give me the Eye and I shall spare your life and the life of your friend." Ector points the dagger at Gisla. "But for the part she played in Laurentia's plan, the girl must die."

"No!" I cry, shifting my body so that it blocks Ector's view of Gisla.

She defiantly shouts over my shoulder, "I'm not afraid of you!"

Ector takes another step forward. "You should be, stupid girl! You should have stayed in Brussels and lived out your natural life as a mere weaver. Instead you involved yourself in matters that are far beyond your comprehension. If I destroyed Laurentia, the most powerful witch in the Low Countries, what do you think I will do to you?"

I hear Gisla mumbling something under her breath and then we all hear Ector cry out in pain. The dagger's blade has turned as red as a hot coal! It clatters to the floor as Ector clutches his scorched palm. "You will pay for that, girl!" he snarls.

Ari takes advantage of the moment. Like a baseball player sliding into home plate, he launches himself at Ector's feet and with his outstretched leg kicks the fallen dagger. It skitters and spins across the chapel's stone floor.

"Enough!" Ector barks. "You pests must be exterminated." He points at the tomb effigy in the center of the chapel and mutters a string of strange words.

Suddenly the stone sculpture of the French knight begins

to stir. His limbs move slowly as if they are stiff from the prayerful pose he has held for the past eight hundred years. But then the knight sits up, swings his legs over the edge of the stone slab, and stands before us. His face is immobile—his unblinking eyes do not move—but the knight seems to see us clearly. He pulls his sword from its sheath and raises his shield, ready for battle.

"What do we do now?" Ari asks.

"Uh—run?" I suggest, backing toward the stairs.

Gisla shakes her head. "We can't abandon the unicorn. That's just what Ector wants us to do."

I hear a strange swishing sound and look more closely at the knight. It's the chain mail under his tunic—it's moving because the knight is...thawing! His entire body is morphing from stone to metal on flesh. His limbs move more freely as he strides toward us with his sword raised above his head.

Behind me I hear Gisla muttering strange words once more. I turn and ask, "What are you doing?"

"Fighting fire with fire," she says with a sly smile.

A second later the tomb effigy at the back of the chapel comes to life as well! Though he has no shield, this warrior wears chain mail from head to toe and his plate armor looks sturdy. He lifts his heavy legs over the edge of his stone sarcophagus and heads straight for the knight with his own sword drawn.

We jump out of the way and press ourselves against the wall of the chapel. Ari and I stare at Gisla in awe. "How did you do that?"

"I may only be a witch's apprentice," she says with a

mischievous smirk, "but I *have* lived in a tapestry for five hundred years. I'm very good at reading lips! I simply repeated the spell Ector used a moment ago."

As the French knight and Spanish count trade blows, we do our best to stay out of their way. The unicorn remains frozen but Ector has to scurry behind the statue of a woman saint to avoid the clanging swords. We huddle in the corner farthest from him and try to come up with a plan.

"Where's the dagger?" I ask.

Ari lies flat on his stomach and points to an ornately carved chest on the other side of the chapel. "Over there!" he cries. "It's beneath that tomb."

"We have to get the dagger before Ector finds it. How do we wake the unicorn?" I ask Gisla. "Maybe we could release it into the park."

She shakes her head. The determined look in Gisla's eyes tells me she's also ready to wage war.

"Ector must be stopped. If we free the unicorn, he will just hunt it down again. The unicorn is safe in its dream state. If you two secure the dagger, I will come up with a way to ensnare Ector."

Just then the knight falls to one knee and cries out, "Fripon!" He holds his shield up as the count whacks it over and over with his sword. Then it's the count's turn to cry out, "Diablo!" as the knight suddenly springs up, using his shield to knock the count back several feet.

Ari and I crouch close to the floor and skirt the stone sarcophagus in the middle of the room so we're closer to the dagger. That also takes us closer to the battle!

"If you can lure them over to the other side of the chapel, I'll crawl under that tomb and grab the dagger," Ari says.

I have no idea how to lure away two men with swords without losing my head. But then, just as I stand up, Ector casts another spell. The battle ends and silence fills the chapel as the knight and count freeze in place.

"I will deal with you myself," Ector growls.

Ari scurries under the chest and stays out of sight. I glance over my shoulder and see Gisla kneeling on the hard stone floor. I keep one eye on Ector and another on Gisla. She raises her hands above her head. Glittering threads of light appear in the space between her fingers and within seconds a golden net materializes. Just as Ector lunges at me, Gisla jumps up and hurls the net at him.

For several seconds Ector struggles against the net, which gives us time to regroup. Ari wriggles out from under the carved stone chest with the bejeweled dagger in his hand. Gisla's net clings to Ector like a spider's web, but it is more irritating than confining. When Ector finally breaks free of the sticky gold strands, he turns on us with even greater fury.

"You were warned! I will show you no mercy now."

Ector opens his arms and tilts his head up toward the vaulted ceiling of the chapel. When his eyes roll back in his head, Gisla urges us to move.

"Stand before the unicorn. Ector wouldn't dare risk harming it," she insists.

But Gisla is wrong. When a sizzling stream of energy

drops down from the ceiling, Ector hurls it at us—not caring that he might strike the unicorn instead.

We duck and the powerful bolt takes a big chunk out of the stone wall of the chapel. Ector summons a second bolt but before he can throw it our way, Ari grabs the frozen knight's shield. He holds it before us and when Ector releases the next bolt, it bounces back and knocks him off his feet. Ector hits the wall behind him and crumples to the floor in a heap of smoldering brocade and velvet.

Ari drops the shield and rubs his arm.

"Are you okay?" Gisla asks him.

When Ari nods, we creep forward to see if Ector is dead. He moans softly and we look at one another uncertainly.

"Should we help him?" I ask my friends.

"He wouldn't help us!" Ari says with contempt. "I vote for putting Ector back in the tapestry where he can't do any harm. Can you do that?" he asks Gisla.

Gisla stares at Ector but says nothing. I think I see tears shining in her eyes.

"This girl's got selective hearing," Ari mutters.

Gisla blinks back her tears and turns to him. "I heard you, Ari. I just need time to think things through. If I put Ector back in the tapestry, he may find his way out again."

I follow Gisla's train of thought and see why she's upset. "We can't kill him," I argue.

"Why not?" Ari asks. "He tried to kill us!"

"That doesn't make it right," I counter.

I take the water bottle out of my knapsack and kneel down beside Ector. Gisla takes off his singed hat and tilts his head back so I can pour some water between Ector's lips. My hand is trembling and water spills all over the place.

We all jump back when Ector suddenly sputters and starts coughing. He opens his eyes and tries to focus on my face. When his gaze falls on the looking drop, he groans and closes his eyes once more.

Ari folds his arms across his chest. "So what are we going to do?" He points at Gisla. "You said Ector had to be stopped."

Gisla shrugs helplessly and looks at me. I crouch next to Ector once more. I hold out the water bottle but he shakes his head so I put it away. I take a deep breath and ask Ector a question: "Why do you want to destroy our world?"

For a long while he says nothing. Ari sighs impatiently and mutters, "This is a waste of time."

Then Ector opens his eyes and speaks in a raspy voice. "You know why. Men murder and enslave their fellow men. Greed corrupts almost every heart. The rich revel in their wealth while the poor starve and suffer. Nations wage wars without end. If you truly believe that love conquers all, join me! Help me open the gate and we shall soon discover whether you are right or wrong, boy."

I bristle but bite my tongue before a mean name comes out of my mouth. Mama says it's disrespectful to call someone out of their name, but Ector doesn't know mine so I start by introducing myself.

"My name is Qing Yuan."

He nods and says, "That's not what others call you, is it? You tell them to call you 'Q' because you are ashamed of your name."

"I am not!" I cry.

"You are," Ector insists. "I see the shame you carry in your heart. You wish you had a different name—and a different family. I can give you both. I can give you everything your heart desires if you help me open the gate."

"You're wrong!" I yell, my cheeks burning with shame. "You don't know what's in my heart! I love my mothers and I love my father, too. I'm proud to be their son!"

Ector makes a slight movement that might be a shrug. "What you want most of all is to be like other children. But you never will be. You'll always stand out. You'll always feel different...unnatural...*alone.*"

I fight the urge to cry and clamp my hands over my ears to shut out Ector's hurtful words. How can he know I've felt that way sometimes? Ari puts his hand on my shoulder. I uncover my ears, blink away my tears, and look up at my friend.

"Don't listen to him, Q," Ari says. "He's just trying to bait you."

Ector shifts his icy gaze and addresses Ari instead of me. "You're no better—hiding the symbol of your faith."

Ari's eyes open in shock. Then his cheeks burn with rage. He pulls the gold Star of David out of his shirt and proudly shows it to Ector. "I'm not hiding anything! Being Jewish is about what you believe, not what you wear."

Ector ignores Ari's words and says with fake sympathy, "I don't blame you, my boy, for hiding what you are. After all the crimes that have been committed against the Jews, why would you oppose me? Don't you want revenge?"

Ari shakes his head. "There are enough devils in the world with you unleashing more! I don't need revenge. And I don't need to prove how strong and resilient my people are—and always will be. I know it in my heart."

Ector twists his lips in disgust and turns to Gisla. "Your mistress filled your head with lies, girl. Laurentia did not save the unicorn—she enslaved it! With your help, she tried to banish the creature to the Shadowlands. She took away its freedom and *you* helped bring about her death!"

Gisla looks both shocked and hurt. While she is defending herself and her mistress, I watch Ector and notice his strength returning. He is no longer slumped against the wall and his hands are tightly clenched into fists.

Ari crouches beside me and whispers in my ear. "Ector's feeding off our anger! We've got to stay cool."

We stand up and signal to Gisla to stop arguing with Ector. She clearly has plenty more she wants to say, but she folds her arms across her chest and keeps quiet for now.

"What's the plan?" Ari asks me.

Suddenly I remember what Dr. Khan said about the inscription on my mirror. "*You* felt unloved as a boy, didn't you, Ector? What you claim to see in *my* heart is really what's inside of yours."

"Careful, boy," Ector warns.

I can tell I've touched a nerve. I glance at Ari and he nods, urging me on.

"Did *you* feel lonely as a child? Were you ashamed of *your* family? Or were they ashamed of *you*?"

Ector is still too weak to stand but he leans toward us like a dog straining against its leash. "I come from one of the wealthiest, most respected families in Brussels!" he barks. "I wanted for nothing as a child."

"But your father still sent you away," Gisla says in a smug voice. "He doted on your older brother, not you. Your mother hoped you would become a priest, but the monks at the monastery knew that would never come to pass. Even as a boy you were selfish."

"I may not have been my father's favorite," Ector admits, "but in the end I was his only living heir."

"Yes—Laurentia told me how you poisoned your brother. Just as you poisoned her!" Gisla cries.

Ari squeezes Gisla's arm and she reins in her rage once more. Ector leans his head back against the wall and sneers at us.

"Look at you—three little cowards. Afraid to do what you know must be done. You would never survive in my glorious new world."

"I'm glad I have a conscience," I tell Ector. "Our world is far from perfect, but it's still worth fighting for."

Ari and Gisla nod in agreement and I go on. "Want to know what's really in my heart, Ector? Not shame—hope. You want us to believe that nothing will ever change, but we know that's not true. You may have given up on humankind but we haven't. The three of us have only known one another a little while but look what we have accomplished— we defeated you, a powerful wizard!"

"And we saved the last unicorn," Ari adds.

"You underestimated us," Gisla says.

A malicious grin spreads across Ector's face. "Just as you underestimated me!"

He opens one of his fists and hurls a crackling ball of blinding white light at Gisla. I jump in front of her and the ball explodes in my chest. I hear Ari shout "No!" Then I feel myself falling and everything goes dark.

9

I wake up to a kaleidoscope of colors. Gisla dabs at my face with a damp cloth and Ari leans over me, calling my name.

I blink several times and the stained glass windows of the chapel come into focus. I realize I am lying on the hard stone floor. With my friends' help, I manage to sit up.

"What happened?" I ask groggily.

"You destroyed Ector!" Ari says excitedly.

"I did? How?"

"The Moor's Eye," Gisla says.

I reach for the mirror and feel a deep ache in my chest. Whatever Ector threw didn't damage the looking drop but it definitely left a bruise.

"You saved Gisla," Ari tells me, "and the looking drop saved you."

I glance around the chapel. The knight and the count are still frozen in battle, but Ector is nowhere to be found.

Gisla points to a pile of ash on the chapel floor. "That's all that's left of him," she explains.

"And the unicorn?"

"I'll break its trance when you've had time to recover,"

Gisla tells me.

"I'm ready to go," I say.

They help me stand up. Sunlight is no longer streaming through the tall windows of the chapel. "How long was I knocked out?" I ask.

"Quite a while," Ari replies. "I'm just glad you're okay. This has been an amazing adventure but I am definitely ready to go home!"

Gisla handles the clean-up by herself. She unfreezes the knight and the count before ordering them back to their tombs. They sheath their swords and lie down just as they were before enchantment brought them back to life.

Next Gisla wakes the unicorn by whispering something in its ear. She strokes its mane for a little while and then steps back to give the unicorn room to stand. It neighs once or twice, shakes its head, and gets to its feet.

"Kom met mij mee," Gisla says and the unicorn seems to nod before following her out of the chapel.

Ari guides us to the exit reserved for staff members. On our way out of the museum, we hear several people yawning loudly and are relived to know that the sleeping spell is starting to wear off.

When we reach the exit, Gisla asks us to wait for a moment. She dashes off but returns just a couple of minutes later.

"I thought maybe you went back for that ugly hat," Ari says.

Gisla laughs. "That itchy thing can stay where it is," she says. "I just had one final spell to cast—a weaving spell my mistress taught me. The tapestries have been restored. Now no one will be unjustly blamed."

Once we get outside, we lead the unicorn into Fort Tryon Park. We find a secluded area shielded by a giant oak tree and some tall hedges. The sun is setting so most people are leaving the park, but we still don't want to attract attention.

"There's something I've been wondering," Ari begins. "Is it a girl or a boy?"

Gisla looks confused. "It's a unicorn."

Ari rolls his eyes. "I know that! But is it male or female?"

Gisla frowns and turns to me for an explanation. I just sigh and say, "What does it matter? The unicorn's safe now. Right?"

Gisla nods and reaches up to lovingly caress the unicorn's long white neck. "Now it's up to me to keep it safe."

"How will you do that?" I ask.

Gisla strokes the creature's cheek. "The unicorn's horn is prized by many. It will never be safe in this world."

Though I'd never want it to be harmed, the thought of losing the beautiful unicorn makes me sad. Then I feel a flash of anger inside of me. Another amazing creature pushed to the brink of extinction by selfish humans.

"In Africa, elephants and rhinos are killed for their horns, too," I tell Gisla. "They stop poachers sometimes by painting the tusks bright pink or sawing them off completely."

"I couldn't imagine stripping the unicorn of its lovely horn," she says. "But there are other possibilities."

"Such as?"

Gisla steps closer and whispers something in the unicorn's ear. Then she takes a few steps back and signals to us to do the same.

"What's she up to now?" Ari whispers.

I just shrug and say, "We'll have to wait and see."

Gisla opens her arms and holds her palms up to the darkening sky. Then she tilts her head back and begins muttering words that definitely aren't English. I listen closely and after a moment realize she's repeating the same string of words over and over again.

Ari gasps and grips my arm. "Look at the unicorn!"

I can hardly believe my eyes. The white hide of the unicorn is turning black! It's as if night itself has swallowed the beautiful creature. Beneath long black lashes, the unicorn's eyes shine like stars. Its horn gleams like polished onyx.

When she finally stops chanting, the unicorn meanders over to Gisla and nuzzles her affectionately.

I watch them for a moment. They seem like old friends. Wherever the unicorn goes next, I suspect Gisla will be going there, too. "You won't go back inside the tapestry, will you?"

Gisla shakes her head. "No. The tapestry was my home for many, many years. But I've missed being a real girl, being three—what did you call it?"

"3D—three dimensional," Ari says.

"Yes. Life is too rich and too full of possibilities to stand back and merely observe."

"Where will you go?" I ask.

Gisla strokes the unicorn's neck and smiles but her eyes look kind of sad. "Into the Shadowlands."

"The Shadowlands? That doesn't sound good. Why don't you stay here with us?"

Ari seconds my idea. "You could go to school. Maybe my uncle could even get you a job at the museum! With everything you know about the Middle Ages, you'd make a great historian."

Gisla smiles but looks unconvinced. "Your world certainly is interesting," she says, "and I have learned much from our time together. But the unicorn and I have been together for centuries—it's like family to me. I don't think I could bear for us to be apart. And the only true sanctuary for the unicorn is in the Shadowlands."

Looking at Gisla as she gently strokes the cheek of the sable unicorn, I can't imagine them living apart either. "You belong together. What will you do there?"

"We will finally be free!" Gisla's smile shrinks a little. "Perhaps I will find Laurentia there with the other esteemed Elders. I long to see my mistress again, but my love for her has never faded. She taught me so much that I feel as if she has been beside me all these years—and will be forever more." Gisla turns and bows to us. "As will both of you. I cannot thank you enough for coming to my aid. You are both brave, and noble, and kind. I will remember you always."

Ari's cheeks turn pink and I can feel mine warming up, too.

"I wish I had my camera," Ari says.

"Will you ever forget this moment?" I ask him. "I know I won't."

"You're right," he replies. "We don't need a photograph. But it would be kind of cool to take a selfie with a unicorn!"

I stop laughing when I notice that Gisla is staring at me.

"The Moor's Eye came to you for a reason," she says solemnly. "Cherish it and keep it safe."

"I will," I promise as I wrap my fingers around the looking drop. "I feel so lucky to have it."

"You are not lucky," Gisla says, shaking her head. "You are *worthy*. If ever I can return the favor and offer my assistance, don't hesitate to call on me."

"How can he do that?" Ari asks. "Should he send you an email? Gisla@shadowlands.com?"

Gisla gives Ari a confused look but despite his corny joke, I was thinking the same thing.

"The Eye will guide you to us," she explains. "Just look into the mirror and let your heart lead you."

I look down at the mirror and see my reflection smiling back at me. I'm not sure just what Gisla means about finding the Shadowlands, but it's reassuring to know we might see her and the unicorn again someday.

"Group hug!" Ari cries.

We throw our arms around each other and hold on tight for a moment. Then Ari and I step back so Gisla can get going.

She makes a soft clucking sound and the unicorn bends its left front leg. Gisla grabs hold of its mane and swings herself onto the unicorn's back. It straightens its leg and stands proudly in the moonlight. Gisla's not a princess but she looks regal as she waves at us. Then she makes another clucking sound and the unicorn rears up on its hind legs before galloping into the night.

10

"What do we do now?" Ari asks me.

"I reach into my pocket and take out my house key. "Now we go home. Time to face the music."

Ari shudders. "We've been gone all day! I think I'd rather face Ector again." He pulls his flip phone out of his pocket and offers it to me. "Want to call your mom?"

"After you," I say.

We start walking back through the park. Ari calls home but has to hold the phone away from his ear when his mom starts yelling. Ma doesn't ream me out but I hear the worry in her voice and that makes me feel just as bad.

Something else is bothering me. Even though we just defeated a villain from the Middle Ages, I have a hard time finding the nerve to ask Ari a question. Finally I take a deep breath and say, "Do you think Ector really could see what's inside our hearts?"

Ari shakes his head. "No way! That loser just saw what he wanted to see."

"I guess…but—"

"But what?" Ari asks.

I stop walking and glance around to see if anyone's

listening. We're at the park entrance, which means we'll be home soon. People are going in and out of the nearby subway station, but it's just the two of us standing on this side of the street. I step out of the circle of light cast by the lamppost. In the shadows I feel safe enough to make a confession.

"That stuff Ector said about me? Some of it's true. Sometimes I *do* wish I could just fit in and be like everyone else."

Ari puts his hand on my shoulder. "Everyone feels that way, Q."

"Even you?" I ask doubtfully.

"Even me," Ari admits. "Though sometimes I feel like I fit in *too* well. My cousins live in Florida and their school has gotten bomb threats! Nothing like that happens to me because I go to public school. I don't stand out anywhere, but my friend Noor does. She's one of the bravest people I know. Last spring some jerk tried to pull off her headscarf while she was on the bus. But she still came to school the next day wearing her hijab."

"I wish I had that kind of courage," I say.

"Well, Noor's just *one* of the bravest people I know," Ari says with a smile. "You're no coward, Q. You proved that today. It doesn't matter if you doubt yourself sometimes. We all do that. Ector was trying to feed our doubts. But we didn't cave—we passed the test."

Looking at it that way makes me feel a bit better. Ari pulls me back into the light and we head on home.

"What are you doing on Monday?" Ari asks.

I shrug. "Since I'm probably going to be grounded, nothing much. You?"

"It's the eclipse, remember? You got viewing glasses?" When I shake my head, Ari grins. "Want to come over and make a viewer with me? I have everything we need."

"That sounds awesome—if Ma says it's okay."

"Tell her it's a science experiment," Ari suggests. "Parents love it when we do anything related to science." He pauses and then asks, "Do you think we should tell our folks what really happened at the museum?"

I think for a moment. I don't want to lie to Ma, but I'm not sure she'd believe me if I told her we saved a unicorn and prevented the apocalypse. "We better not," I say.

Ari nods thoughtfully. "That means we have to come up with another reason for being out so late. Got any ideas?"

By the time we reach our building, Ari and I have agreed upon a story to tell our parents: there was a chemical spill at the museum and the fumes knocked everyone out for several hours.

"Think they'll buy it?" Ari asks as the elevator takes us up to the fifth floor.

"Probably not," I say. The door slides open and we step into the hallway.

"Uncle David will back us up," Ari says optimistically.

"True. But you know what? Even if I get grounded for a month—it was totally worth it." I wait a second and then add, "I'm really glad you were there today, Ari."

"So am I, Q! And you heard what Gisla said about your looking drop—it could guide you to the Shadowlands."

I laugh. "You up for another adventure?"

"You bet!" Ari calls over his shoulder as he heads down the hall to his apartment.

I wait to see Ari let himself in before heading up the stairs. I turn the key in the lock and brace myself for a long lecture from Ma. But just as I close the door behind me, the phone rings. Saved by the bell!

Ma hands me the phone and says, "We need to talk, young man. But you should talk to your father first. He's called twice already this evening."

I take the phone from Ma and give her a quick hug before pressing the talk button.

"Hey, Qing! Where have you been? Your mother was worried about you."

I sink onto the sofa and grin from ear to ear. It feels good to hear my dad's voice, even if he's about to lecture me.

"Hey, Dad. We were at the museum and we, uh…lost track of time." I glance at Ma. She raises one eyebrow skeptically, but then Sophie starts to cry and Ma goes into the other room.

Dad sounds doubtful, too. "You did, huh? The Cloisters must be a pretty special place."

"It sure is!" I exclaim. "I can't wait to go back."

"Your mother tells me the museum director called to apologize for the way you were treated yesterday." There's a pause and then Dad says, "I'm sorry that happened to you, Q. It wasn't right."

"Yeah, it was messed up. But Ari and I figured out what

happened to the tapestry and a friend of ours was able to fix it."

"Really? I'm glad to hear you've already made a few friends in your new neighborhood."

"Ari lives in our building. My other friend was cool, too, but she moved away today." I pause and take a deep breath. "Are you still in jail?" I ask finally.

"No," Dad replies. "I'm home now."

I can hear the relief in his voice. "Did Thandie bail you out?"

Dad laughs. "Actually, she didn't have to. The judge let all the protestors go. She said the police officers at the march shouldn't have arrested people who were just exercising their First Amendment right to assemble peacefully."

"I saw some of those other guys on the news—the angry ones with the red flags. They didn't look peaceful. They looked pretty scary."

Dad sighs. "I won't lie, Q. I *was* scared. But I wasn't alone and that made all the difference."

I think about the way Ari, Gisla, and I worked together to defeat Ector. "It's a lot easier to stand up to a bully when you know someone's got your back," I say.

"It sure is!" Dad replies. There's a pause and then he says, "I'm really sorry our plans for this weekend fell through, Q. I know you were counting on me."

"I'm sorry I didn't come to the phone when you called before. I guess I was disappointed—but only because I really wanted to see you this weekend. Then I read your letter and, well—I'm really proud of you, Dad. You stood

up for what was right. Ari says that makes you a hero, even if you didn't punch a Nazi."

Dad chuckles. "I hope I'll get to meet your new friend when I drive up to New York next weekend."

I jump up off the sofa. "You're still coming?"

"I sure am. The museum director promised to give you a family membership. I'm family, right?"

"Sure! Wow, that's so cool. A membership means we can go to The Cloisters as many times as we want—for free!"

"That's right," Dad says.

"There's so much to see and do there. Ari and I had the most amazing adventure. And it's all because of the looking drop you sent me. Where'd you get it?"

"Thandie and I found it at a flea market," Dad tells me. "I knew right away that it was something you'd like. The man who sold it to us thought it was Turkish."

"Dr. Khan says it's Moorish," I tell him. "She's a curator at the museum. She even translated the inscription for me: "A Believer is the mirror for a Believer.""

"Interesting," Dad muses. "What do you think that means, Q?"

I consider his question for a moment. Then I say, "It means you should show your best self to others—and look for the best in them, too. But you should also be honest about what's in your heart. That way no one can turn your fears against you."

I can't see my dad's face, but I can tell he's smiling. "Those are wise words, Q," he says. "You know, I joined that march because I want the world to be a safe place for our family," Dad says. "I want you and your sister to grow up without being afraid of anything or anyone."

"I know," I tell him. "But I can help make the world a better place. I've got everything I need—good friends, a family that loves me, and a little bit of magic!"

THE END

Discussion Guide

1. Q thinks his family is "unique." What makes your family different or special? When do you feel most proud of your family?

2. Why doesn't Q want to talk to his father after he is arrested? If Q wrote a letter instead, what do you think he should say to his dad?

3. If you could make a tapestry that showed you doing something in your community, how would it look? Where would you want that tapestry to be displayed?

4. Who was Mansa Musa and what made him the richest man ever? Do you think Genghis Khan was a great leader? Find an important woman who lived during the Middle Ages (5th - 15th century).

5. Sometimes adults try to protect kids by not talking about current events that might be upsetting or frightening. Is this the right thing to do? What advice would you give to kids who feel worried about things they see or hear in the news?

6. Q's father attends a peace march to stand up for what he believes. How do you express your beliefs? Do you wear special clothing? Do particular

symbols represent your values? What do you do when someone disagrees with your point of view or disrespects your beliefs?

7. "A Believer is the mirror of a Believer." What does this mean to you? Ector wants the Moor's Eye for himself, and yet he finds it hard to look at his own reflection—why?

8. Learn more about the Moors and dhimmis in Al-Andalus. How did early Muslim rulers encourage tolerance of religious differences? Now learn about the Jewish scholar Maimonides. What was life like for him in Córdoba?

9. Gisla misses Laurentia very much but is thankful for the lessons she learned as her apprentice. Who has taught you important or valuable skills? How do you apply those lessons in your life?

10. Imagine you are the curator of your very own museum. How will you build a collection of objects to display? What type of exhibit would be most interesting to you and your friends, family, or community?

Afterword

I've been a medieval geek ever since I was a kid. One of my favorite books, *The Magic Cave*, was by Brooklyn author Ruth Chew; two White children free Merlin from an ancient oak tree and help him retrieve artifacts from the Brooklyn Museum. In high school I wrote my senior thesis on *The Mists of Avalon*, a feminist retelling of the Arthurian legend. In college, I took courses on medieval European history. No one who looked like me ever appeared in the narratives I so admired, and I accepted the Middle Ages as a wondrous, White world.

When my college roommate Lucy went to New York City with her sorority sisters, she returned with a present for me: a print of *The Unicorn in Captivity* from The Met gift shop. Lucy told me about The Cloisters and I vowed I would visit it myself one day. As a girl, it had been acceptable for me to dream of castles and unicorns, but I learned as a teen to hide my love of elves, fairies, and mythical creatures. I was Black, and the realm of magic—so I was told—wasn't meant for me (unless I was trying to be White). But Lucy simply took me as I was; instead of sneering or shaming me as others had done, Lucy encouraged my interests and assured me I had the right to imagine myself in any world.

I discovered as an adult what I had never known as a child: that people of color were an integral part of the Middle Ages, and medieval history wasn't confined to Europe. Friends directed me to *Medievalpoc*, which uses social media to provide a steady supply of artwork featuring Africans in Europe, and while watching television shows like *Vikings*, *The Last Kingdom*, and *Game of Thrones*, I began to develop a novel about Black women Vikings.

I also reevaluated the stories I loved as a child, and searched for ways to subvert storytelling conventions that figure "black magic" as something to be defeated. I started writing stories that became the City Kids series, which centers kids of color in adventures that combine history, social justice, and magic.

When I was hired to teach a summer creative writing class for Uptown Stories in Washington Heights, I scheduled a field trip to The Cloisters; it was nearby, one of my favorite museums, and a great site to teach kids how to write historical fantasy. The class was called "Ghosts, Portals, and Time Travelers," and I wrote *The Phantom Unicorn* to serve as an example of speculative fiction for my students to consider. After the tragic violence in Charlottesville, VA, I also wanted a way to bring kids into the conversation about memorials and the sometimes problematic ways we (mis)remember the past.

I shared a couple of chapters of *The Phantom Unicorn* with my students and truly valued their feedback. My first visit to The Cloisters was a magical experience, and it was gratifying to witness that same enthusiasm and sense of wonder in my students as we explored the museum together. We were treated courteously by The Cloisters' staff; Q's encounter with the security guard is purely fictional, but I wrote that scene because children of color are sometimes heavily surveilled and made to feel unwelcome in museums.

I am grateful to Kate Reuther and Glendaliz Camacho for giving me the opportunity to teach the amazing young writers at Uptown Stories. During our closing celebration I met Cheryl Seraile Yam, and she provided me with valuable insights as the mother of three biracial children. This is my first time writing about a Jewish character and I greatly appreciate the assistance provided by my friends Ruben Brosbe, Laura Atkins, and Roni Natov. The Moor's Eye in this story was inspired by an actual "looking drop" given to me by my thoughtful friend Janine Macbeth. I very much appreciate the insights provided by my fellow author Rukhsana Khan and Prof. Amina Steinfels; I look forward to conducting further research on magic and the Moors. I am also grateful that my former student Bonnie Sheppard gave me Adolfo Salvatore Cavallo's book *The Unicorn Tapestries at the Metropolitan Museum of Art*, which helped immensely. This is my fifth collaboration with UK illustrator Charity Russell, and I thank her for using her talent to create a beautifully inclusive magical world.

The City Kids series represents the books I wish I'd had as a child. In this particular era of rising intolerance, it's more important than ever that we feed our imagination so that we can dream—and build—a nation where the contributions of all our community members are valued.

~ Zetta Elliott
Brooklyn, NY
October 16, 2017

About the Author

Zetta Elliott is the award-winning author of over twenty books for young readers. She lives in Brooklyn and loves museums, the Middle Ages, and magical creatures.

Learn more at www.zettaelliott.com

About the Illustrator

Charity Russell lives in Bristol, England with her husband and two children. She has a Master's Degree in Illustration and Design from The University of Sunderland. She loves all things bookish and receiving hand-written letters in the post.

www.charityrussell.com

Explore other titles in the City Kids series!

Best friends Carlos and Tariq love their block, but Barkley Street has started to change. The playground has been taken over by older boys, which leaves Carlos and Tariq with no place to call their own. They decide to turn the yard of an abandoned brownstone into their secret hang-out spot. Carlos and Tariq soon discover, however, that the overgrown yard is already occupied by an ancient phoenix! When the Pythons try to claim the yard for their gang, the magical bird gives the friends the courage to make a stand against the bullies who threaten to ruin their beloved neighborhood.

Summer vacation has just begun and Dayshaun wants to spend Saturday morning playing his new video game. But Dayshaun's mother has other plans: she volunteers at a nearby community garden and that means Dayshaun has to volunteer, too. When Dayshaun puts on his grandfather's grubby old gardening hat, something unexpected happens— the hands of time turn backward and Dayshaun finds himself in the free Black community of Weeksville during the summer of 1863! While helping the survivors of the New York City Draft Riots, Dayshaun meets a frail old man who entrusts him with a precious family heirloom. But will this gift help Dayshaun find his way back to the 21st century?

Zaria has dreamed of England for as long as she can remember—according to the many novels she's read, everything magical happens there! When her grandfather suffers a stroke, Zaria and her mother head to London to help care for him. Zaria reads fantastic tales to her grandfather every afternoon, and she's thrilled to discover that her cousin Winston shares her love of wands, wizards, and mythical creatures. But Zaria soon finds that life in London is actually quite ordinary—until she goes on a day trip to nearby Windsor Castle. There Zaria meets two extraordinary ghosts who need help finding their way back to the African continent they once called home.

Learn more about the City Kids series at www.zettaelliott.com

CPSIA information can be obtained
at www.ICGtesting.com
Printed in the USA
FSHW011227190721